STREETS 1970

Merle Molofsky

IPBOOKS.net
International Psychoanalytic Books

A Division of International Psychoanalytic Media Group

Copyright © 2015 Merle Molofsky
Printed in the USA

International Psychoanalytic Books (IPBooks),

 25–79 31st Street Astoria, NY 11102
Online at: http://www.IPBooks.net

Cover art by Hailey Doran.

This is a work of fiction. All names, characters, places and incidents
either are the product of the author's imagination or are used fictitiously.
Any resemblance to actual persons, living or dead, is coincidental.

ISBN: 978-0-9906613-2-0

Library of Congress Control Number: 2014959623

Dedicated with gratitude to my brother,
Jonathan Molofsky, my "ideal reader," always
sensitive, responsive, appreciative, and encouraging.

Streets 1970: An Introduction

Are there perennial truths? Truths we have to find over and over again if we want to feel real, if we want to know what human living is all about? Well I think the answer is, most likely, yes. So where do we find such truths? Philosophy asks the question—sometimes it attempts an answer; empirical science tells us about the makeup of our everyday world, not the human truths on how to live in it. Psychology tries to clear the road so we can get somewhere . . . we generally need road clearing. If I had to pick one area of human thought that helps in this quest it would be, not exclusively, but primarily, literature. Poetry, plays, dialogues, novels—the play of words upon our ears, our memories and our souls convey the becoming human condition that defines our lives.

Recently, I heard a rather insightful remark, "beware the unloved". I interpreted "beware" as . . . *take note of . . . be attentive to.* The unloved are tormented, they never know if they have done enough; frequently they do not even know what they are doing.

Have we all been loved enough? Not too many of us. But that is ultimately not just a private experience. We are, after all, all connected; we are, in some inexplicable way, one—we humans. The more we come to know our own unloved areas the more we can feel those areas in others. The more we live the human experience. Some people fulfill their dreams, others fear to have them—still others lose their dreams to money, to fear, to convention, to drugs—the list goes on. In this remarkably well-written and engaging novel, Molofsky tells of those who have lost their dreams to drugs. But this novel explores more than that. Good and evil—meaning versus no meaning—sex, love and self-search are made vivid with an acuity of perception that raises the story line to the perennial quest to know the human enterprise. Molofsky's extraordinary skill as a writer is such that there is no need for a linear development of plot; time is a tertiary experience in this novel. The author happens to be a psychoanalyst; this novel was written, however, in her late twenties, many years prior to her present profession. It has a vitality of youth, without the inter-space of psychological categorizations to take away from the immediacy of encounter.

Naught is good nor evil but that thinking makes it so. . . . A philosophical truth? Psychological insight? A guideline for understanding? Unloved people usually hurt themselves—many times they hurt others—not necessarily sacrificing their innocence in the process. In order to see the possibility of innocence one has to describe, not judge, diagnose, preach, or reform. One has to look with innocence, so to speak, if one wants to know what is really happening. Molofsky, accomplished and recognized poet that she is, enables us to look this way. She lets us touch the characters along with her and in the touching we learn about life and death, about how and if we can ever judge another. I am not suggesting some existential vacuity—not at all. There is something more significant here; this storyteller never gets in the way of her story or her characters. Molofsky writes with ease, with an engaging lyric flow, with a rapidity that carries us along, not sure where we will end up.

But we end up not only knowing and liking, or, maybe not liking her characters or her plot; we end up, either way, having to ask ourselves some basic questions about life and death—about sex, love and violence—about yearning—about judgment and non-judgment. The Greek philosopher Solon reminds us to judge no one until his or her death. Molofsky heeds this advice, she does not judge, when the judging would be easy. Rather she helps us experience; helps us take note of those unloved. For every human being who loses his or her life to whatever—we all lose part of ourselves. But that is a reflective philosophical observation. Molofsky offers the same truth without the burden of saying it. And that's what makes her the exceptionally engrossing writer she is.

We all have a leaning toward seeing the world we want, more than the world we have. What to do? We run back to stories—ever since our youth, our collective youth as well as our personal individual youth—and we read or someone reads to us. And, if we are lucky and if we are ready, we find the world anew—even for just a moment. We touch other's lives and in the touching we feel our own. *Streets 1970* gave me such a moment. I wish it for you as well.

Gerald J. Gargiulo
Stamford, Connecticut

CONTENTS

STREETS 1970

DOREEN'S LAMENT

Douglas, dark stream, blue veins roaring with black gaelic life, white joy cutting through underflesh tunnels bringing frozen silence, dark stream feeding flesh and mind, Douglas, while the spirit shrivels, while the spirit dies.

Now I'm just a poor ignorant girl so I'm asking all you philosophers and other wise men whether the soul lives on after the body is gone. And if it does, if the soul dies first, does it get reborn when the body dies? And if the soul does get reborn, will it get the same mindblast from outer space when the radio plays? Is there rock music in heaven, Father? Hey Mister DeeJay, yeah yeah yeah, would you play "This is Dedicated to the One I Love". Douglas, dark stream, memory of corrupt black gaelic blood lightened with white joy, this all-night radio mindblast from outer space, hey it's for you, man. You goddamn dead man. I know, Father, I know, all you wise men, gurus, and philosopher kings, that I'm asking some hard questions. The questions are hard because . . .I don't know. The questions have always been hard but now they're getting harder and I am just a poor ignorant girl, learned all I know from the deejay show on the radio . . . you know. Like the man said, mmm, dig it.

I'm sitting here on half a load of very dynamite shit, waiting for a message from the radio and thinking about Douglas the dead man. I went down to the morgue to identify the body and it looked like Douglas, but it wasn't really him, because the man I knew was locked in the prison of his dreams and his bloodstream, fighting to escape, and this dead man had escaped. There was no man there, just forsaken flesh. I said yes, this is Douglas, but there was no Douglas anywhere, except maybe the knot beginning to twist and rage inside me. The man said what about funeral arrangements and I had to laugh, I walked out laughing. Douglas always walked on the outside, you know, where you can hear the laughter, the constant laughter, and now I can hear the laughter too. Man, I don't want to know where they ditch the body. They can feed it to the birds. I want to find Douglas, I want to walk on the outside with that laughter, I want to feel the rage and still the pain. . . .

Douglas used to say he was a student of the mythology of pain. Douglas said that pain was like reading a book towards and away from the center, with an intolerable build-up and no climax. What did he mean by curiously involuted? Pain is curiously involuted, he said. He played with pain. I never saw a junkie play with pain before. He'd sit there with his stuff and he'd stare at it for a long time. Everybody would have gotten off and he'd still be there, sweating, staring at his works. He'd cook the stuff down and fill up his works and slide the needle into his vein and wait. No one could bear to watch him. He'd wait and he'd be sweating and he'd ask people questions in a choked-up voice. Questions about themselves, where they came from and about their childhood, and then he'd ask questions about life and god, and people would answer him because they knew that if he liked an answer then he'd get off and not fuck their heads around with questions. Later when he was straight and the pain was gone he'd always say did I do the wrong thing? but then he didn't expect an answer and no one else thought that way anyhow. Did I do the wrong thing? When, Douglas? What wrong thing? When did you do it? I understood what he was talking about but I didn't know how to talk that kind of talk. He was talking about a whole lot of years, that I do know, not that one shot. Even when he was studying the mythology of pain he never meant that partic- ular shot. Once when no one answered the questions right he shot his stuff across the room against the wall. I had to go out and score again. You can't just let a man suffer like that.

Douglas told me he used to be an altar boy and that's why he liked hippies, because of the incense. He used to smoke weed with a lot of freaks and Douglas would listen to the Kyrie Eleison on their phonograph and smell their incense and ask them to talk about God. We would smoke weed and I would watch the frantic people and not understand. I didn't mind. They didn't understand either. Then we'd go back home and score again and Douglas would ask the junkies about god too, his hair still smelling of incense. No one knew about god. Our habits got too big and I kicked on methadone but Douglas just kicked. He said it didn't matter whether he was stoned or withdrawing, they were both highs. He just didn't want to die without being a junkie. Stoned or sweating it, but still a junkie. As soon as he kicked he shot up again. Me too.

Douglas sat on the edge of the bed unraveling his sweater. I asked him why he was unraveling the sweater.

I have to destroy something and I don't want it to be you.

I don't know why I got so mad but I did. I started to scream at him and he knocked me down and sat on top of me with his hand over my mouth and told me in a low even voice everything that I had been when he met me and everything I had become. I degraded you he kept saying. I degraded you. He remembered a lot of things we had done, and yeah, it was all for junk, and he kept saying how degrading it all was. Then he said he was going out to score. Now he had already done a lot of stuff, he was stoned, and I said how high do you have to get. I don't know, he said, I've never been that high. Then he started to pull on the sweater but it was half unraveled so he went out without it. He died shooting ten bags in a hallway down the street.

Oh the rainbow glories I had seen in that dark rushing stream, the pools and eddies and waterfalls, the blackness and the rush that stirred in the blood of my man, and now the stream is still, frozen and clean of all madness and delight.

Let the birds eat him, let his bones gleam white, let the snow fall upon them, for he walked on the outside with the sound of laughter and he died a white death, his dark mind silenced, permanently high.

I put a spell on you, Douglas, I am putting a radar beam on your high, I'm tracking your mind no matter how high you fly mavourneen, mo mhuirnin, cause you dead, daddy, and you left me here behind. Ain't no mountain high enough, babe, to keep you from me. Mmm, dig it.

I'm going to kick. Tomorrow. Tonight I'm going to listen to the radio (mindblast!) and chase an arctic dream, I'm going to dedicate all these songs to the one I love. Even the song I don't recognize . . . that tuneless string of sound (laughter!) that they keep playing over and over and over . . . I'm going to shoot my last shot tonight. So I can kick. I'm not stupid. I've been around. I heard Douglas ask the questions. I was there when he screamed that some one was slipping the notes from underground, a page a day, underneath his door. I'm going to shoot ten bags, maybe fifteen, I don't know how much. The radio hasn't sent me the message yet. But Douglas, I'm going to get so high, so loose, so high . . .

IN THE GARDEN I

On a grassy knoll surrounded by a pine forest free of underbrush lay a glass coffin. Dressed in a brown leather jacket and worn jeans and heavy boots, Douglas slept dreamlessly in the garden, not breathing, served up rare, under glass. Douglas, mythical and dead, in a corner of paradise, where no insects crawled or flew, and where larks and hummingbirds and yellowbellied sapsuckers hovered in the air or perched, shitless, on tree branches. Birdsong filled the air, rich fugues that anticipated the flute, the violin, the trained soprano castrato. Upon sun-dappled meadows the lion and the lamb lay down together, and cherubs rode plump and naked upon the long-lost supertooth tigers, ecstatic in pre-history. About the glass coffin peacocks strolled, majestic and multi-eyed, their tails permanently spread in sexual potency, viewing paradise blindly from behind and rending the air with their banshee shrieks. In the distance violet mountains towered. On the other side of the mountains, invisible to Eden, lay Satan's realm, where birds of prey spread their wide expanse of wing and croaked infernal warnings to those below, their droppings falling like bombs, sulphurous and aflame. But that was another time, another place, and Douglas lay unawakened, unaware, in Paradise, while his eternal fate was being discussed, as innocent as he had been alive on earth while his fate was being decided there.

Around the coffin five figures gathered, not as mourners but as judges, and wearing not the traditional black, the executioner black, of either role. Three women stood together on one side, two men on the other. The two men were dressed as monks in saffron robes, their feet bare, their heads shaven. One was plump and smooth and smug, his robe spotless, his hands manicured, his feet pedicured, the other thin and dirty and derelict, his sharp, bitter, broken-veined face betraying a proclivity for hard spirits. Of the three women, the eldest was dressed in layers of long, threadbare dresses, a seedy black coat, a fur boa that had sustained the ephemeral life of many a moth, rolled stockings, thick white sweat socks, shoes with their toes cut out, and violet-tinted sunglasses. She gummed her mouth incessantly, and the few teeth remaining to her were snagged and blackened. The second woman, of middle years, was unusually tall and strong-bodied, her hips and shoulders wide, her breasts full, her small head with closely trimmed nappy hair erect, thrown back, her spirit so used to dwelling comfortably in a comfortable, life-capable body that she seemed naked despite her thin, ill-cut faded yellow cotton housedress. The third woman, the youngest, scarcely more than a child, wiggled and squirmed, her flowering body barely contained by the white ruffled long-sleeved see-through blouse, the open red imitation red leather vest, the short tight matching red skirt she was wearing. Her stockings were silvery, her high-heeled shoes glittered like gold. When she walked she pranced, when she stood still she balanced on one hip, the other jutting forward. She chewed gum and reached constantly for cigarettes, which she did not have with her.

Gathered before the glass coffin, before the young lean street body, were two Zen priests, Shogen the plump and Mumon the lean, and the three fates, Sister Calliope of Times Square, the crone; Sister Esta of Brooklyn, the nymph; and Sister Silvia of Eighth Avenue, the maiden; New York territory assigned. All five had entered Douglas's mind when he had been alive, summoned by him, perhaps, invaders, perhaps, but familiar with his secrets, with the unveiled dusty corners, the dark spidery recesses, that he himself had glimpsed, had known in terror and exultation. And now he was dead, and remained unawakened in Paradise, while his soul wandered unconscious in limbo, waiting to be called to form, to suffer in hell, to delight in heaven, or to be sent, reborn, to earth, with the faint promise of union, of nirvana, of dissolution into the original universal mind. His last thought, unbidden, hovered over the coffin, formless, a mist, a tentative question that proclaimed, at last, at last, at last. . . .

God's drama, each fragment of God's life living the tragicomedy designed with the first breath of the creation, God's drama . . . every moment is in the present tense, time is a cosmic joke but death puts everything back in perspective, a curtain between drama, the theatre a heartbeat with periodic silences in which something else, non-sound, might be heard. . . .

In a small corner of Paradise Douglas sleeps, unawakened by the chill cry of a peacock, by the stern voices discussing his eternity. Eternity is his . . . he sleeps on.

Shogen walks with firm, delicate steps upon the springy grass his toes curling blissfully, caressing the tender green blades.

— He studied under me. I know him well. I found him stubborn, rebellious, intractable. He substituted callousness for detachment, cheap paradox for insight search, self-aggrandizement for loving-kindness. I accuse him of helping to murder a child, of pandering his woman, of corrupting the innocent, of robbery, of complicity in the murder of an old man. He never renounced his sins, but waited stolidly for the next occasion to rob, to take life, to corrupt life. He denied me, mocked me, abandoned my teachings and the holy way. He saw nothing; he was a fool. He deserves nothing but life; I suggest that he be reborn in the body of a woman, to suffer a woman's destiny, that he might learn compassion for the innocent. —

Douglas lies asleep, the gentle sun gilding his face, finding golden flecks upon the thin skin of his eyelids. His lips are parted, pale and soft, untroubled by the intake and output of life's breath. Sister Silvia stands by the coffin and studies his face through the glass. She twists a lock of her platinum hair about her pinky; she seems to regret past action that she has taken and not perfectly understood.

Well, he ain't exactly a saint. I mean, he never really understood anything he was doing, did he? But he never lied. He may have been wrong about a couple of things, but he never lied. He was like a mirror, in a way, empty of intrinsic image, if you get my meaning, but offering a true reflection to those who looked for themselves within him. I don't see no sense for him to be reborn as a woman. I mean, he was kinda passive, you know, he didn't make a claim for himself, for his own identity. He lived for others, not for himself. He was like a sacrifice. Hell, he was even Christ-like. Don't get me wrong. I knew from the start he was no Christ, but he was Christ-like. I don't think he should be reborn at all. He really had it in those few short years he lived. He's just about ready to get off the wheel. A little time served in hell, a taste of heaven, and then the unknown. That's what I think.

She stands there, undecided, ready to cast a new vote, ready to opt for paradise alone, moved by a certain beauty, a lean hardness of leather jacket, a soft yielding openness that is death. She remembers her hatred of him, and is ashamed. But she has so much time before her, and a little time served in hell seems infinitesimal and necessary compared to an eternity of nullity. So though she reconsiders she says nothing. A woman—she claims the few woman's prerogatives she has and manipulates them with finess — she can always change her mind later, if things go too badly for her protegé.

Shogen is offended. He is old and wise; his sleek round body and untroubled brow bear witness to a life well-spent, an orderly, virtuous existence in which virtue is its own reward and is evident in a certain prosperity and well-being. He resents this chit of a girl, this slut, this womanchild with the flames of hellfire burning between her legs. He spoke first because he recognized that the others would yield to him, in deference to his inner grace and steady wisdom, and that this hussy, so young in years and old in vice, dared to immediately contradict him, is almost more than he can bear. Yet he is well-disciplined; a sage does not lose his poise, his inner peace, his well-nurtured serenity in the face of stupid obstinacy. He rubs his hands together, a complacent smile upon his oily face.

— Well, well, little sister — he begins, — it seems you are not unmoved by his manly beauty, his elegance of form, his piteous youth. Indeed, is he not a flower, perfectly shaped, exquisitely colored, cut off in its prime? Perhaps it does not matter that this flower exudes a subtle poison, that its over-rich perfume is imbued with the odors of decay within, that this thing of beauty is harmful to mankind. In your lack of experience you perhaps would eat shiny red berries, luscious and ripe, only to curl up in agony a few moments later, dying of some subtle poison unleashed by your greed. He is beautiful, true, but he is corrupt. Dwell less on his innocence of expression as he lies here. He is dead, he is beautiful, he can do no harm. Ah, but those sinewy limbs, when activated by the breath of life, performed heinous crimes, those sweetly pouting lips kissed promiscuously and then turned from their object of pleasure. Think again, little sister, and do not let your sensuality cloud your judgment. —

He turns away, satisfied, and plucks a flower from the black earth and inhales its scent. In a moment the flower disintegrates in his hands, and a fresh blossom nods anew in the same spot in which the first flower grew. This is Paradise.

Sister Calliope and Mumon draw close to one another. They understand one another in their heavy mantle of age, in their seamed faces that tell tales of vices and relinquishings. They are gossiping now, telling tales out of school, reminiscing, laughing, forgetful of the motionless body under glass, awaiting reanimation. There is all the time in the world for them, for him. If they were to spend centuries, eons, in chitchat, he still would have an eternity before him. They are not unmoved by his plight; merely realistic, having long ago cracked the mystery of time and found it just another inanity, another infantile joke of the Creator, who himself has long ago sought and found another dimension to horse around in.

> I don't know, — Sister Silvia mutters sullenly, kicking at a pebble. — I just don't know. — She looks to Sister Calliope for spiritual guidance; Sister Calliope, however, is looking to Mumon, coy, coquette to the end, needing no spiritual guidance at all, giving none. Butterflies, in brilliant confusion of color, their wings powdery soft, descend upon Sister Calliope, providing a gay mantle, coat of many colors, so

that she looks a saint in stained glass emblazoned upon a house of worship for women to adore and confide their woes and guilt to.

— Ah, — Shogen purrs, — your sense of charity is rewarded. Perhaps I too should reconsider. —

He draws aside, ostentatiously, to meditate. It seems as if swarms of hornets, a murder of crows, might embrace him, a sign to emphasize his hypocritical unctuousness, but this is Paradise, and all that could happen is that butterflies do not embroider his aura of grace. He is, after all, blessed, and at home in Eden.

Mumon lets his black and glittering eyes slither from Shogen, roly-poly cross-legged upon the carpet of grass, to Sister Calliope, frail, happy, her wrinkled eyelids batting over her diamond-pale blue eyes, watering with joy, her lips puckering in a flirtatious, snaggle-toothed smile, and then focuses his attention, his obsidian gaze, upon Sister Silvia, forlorn and wistful, her hands plunging into the gossamer weave of butterflies, absent-mindedly toying with her nipples, as she is wont to do when she is lost in thought. He feels constrained to say something, but he knows that there is really nothing to say, that he is a teacher who knows nothing, and that nothing cannot be taught, not even in Eden.

— Nothing to make a fuss about, — he finally snaps.
— He was just a junkie, that's all. He lived like a junkie and he died like a junkie. Nothing very unusual about that. —

Sister Esta is standing to one side, contemplating both the casket, the lifeless form within it, and the little knot of arguing saints. She is scornful, skeptical, yet affectionate; motherly, one might say, as one might say of her every gesture, for motherhood is engrained within her. She bears children professionally, raises them with instinctive ease, and sends them out into the world with genial unconcern, for there always will be a new brood to lavish her love upon. She has born several hundred children and is still in her prime.

— You all sound like a bunch of little children, — she purrs, shaking her head from side to side. — You never gonna get things done this way. No one's really concentrating on this thing. You are making this into a game, and everyone's trying to win it. Now just because we know him well we have the right, the obligation, to judge his soul, and we can't let our personal feelings about him enter into this thing. We got to get a little organization going down here. We can't get bogged down in good and evil, for one thing. That's just an ego trip, you folks oughta know that. No more talk about sin, first off. We gotta figure out if he was enlightened, for one thing. Now if he got enlightened, then there's no doubt about it. Nirvana, no ifs or buts. Whether he chooses to be reborn out of a sense of loving-givingness is his own business. Now if the boy ain't enlightened, then we gotta think about heaven. If he fulfilled his humanity then heaven it is. If he died with a sense of guilt, and I ain't saying whether he died guilty or innocent, which is a value judgment, which we all know we are not empowered to make, as good and evil is a metaphysician's concern, not a saint's, whether he felt guilty, whether his mind, body, and soul craves a taste of agony, well then we oblige the child with a couple hundred years of hell. If he died truly confused, with nothing on his mind and everything unsettled like, then he gets reborn. It that is what we decide, we worry about what he gets reborn as later. It's been my experience that you let the dead pick their own incarnation. I mean what better way to learn than to make your own mistakes. Ain't that the truth now? —

Mumon and Sister Calliope stare at Sister Esta with bleary eyes, reluctant to give up their covert flirtation and get on with the business at hand. Sister Silvia regards the older woman with serious respect bordering on awe. Only Shogen remains unmoved, for he is locked in meditation. Sister Esta stomps her foot impatiently. — I know you-all like it here in this garden, but you can't forget your duty. You didn't come here to play, you know. You can come back here any old time you want, for a vacation, or whatever, whenever you want. So you can lay off that phony meditation, Shogen, cause I just know you listening to every word I'm saying. And Sister Calliope, you ought to be ashamed of yourself, at your age, coming on to that man the way you do, and him a priest. And how about it, Mumon? What kind of priest are you anyway? —

Mumon flashes Sister Esta a mischievous grin, with a sharp and lingering appraisal of her body, a long roll of his glinting eyes that takes her in from head to toe, with appropriate pauses as he rests his eyes on some particularly charming feature.

—A strange type of priest, my love, — he drawls. He winks at her and licks his lips, his lechery daring, even outrageous. Sister Silvia giggles. Sister Calliope, not really offended, for she is practical in her wisdom, lays a possessive claw upon his withered arm nonetheless. Shogen, however, is not amused. His posture of meditative ease stiffens. He begins to chant, a succession of open vowels, slightly diphthongized, nasal, and loud, quite loud. The peacocks, moved by his invocation of a godhead, screech with him.

— If that man levitates or pulls any other such shit while we got business to do I'm gonna put him out of the saint business if it's the last thing I do in this incarnation, — Sister Esta mutters. She paces back and forth upon the springy grass, swinging her hips, frowning. Mumon is watching her with an appreciation beyond aesthetics, as she works up her energies. Her eyes take on a cat-yellow light, her breasts bob heavily as she paces, and everyone steps back from her, giving her room, as she traces her patterns upon the ground. Only Shogen remains unconcerned, chanting louder and louder his drone, and at the moment that he begins to rise in the air, still cross-legged, his chant becomes a croak, and he flops down to earth again, transformed, a small greenbrown toad, his long legs flopping out of a pretzeled posture and propelling him in angry leaps about the coffin. In mid-leap he once more is transformed into a man, and sprawls with much lack of dignity upon the grass. As he rises, sputtering and fuming, Sister Esta extends a regal hand. — Before you go getting your bowels in an uproar, I think you better just calm yourself down and pay attention in this here court. You can't just meditate while you got responsibilities. You owe him your full attention, now he's gone and got himself dead. —

Shogen smoothes his robes, runs his hands over the sheen of his bald head. He casts covert glances of fury at Sister Esta, but does not dare confront her, not now. She has the powers on her side. They all resume their moody contemplation of the still figure preserved so well under glass.

A hush falls upon the garden. The skies here never darken with clouds, for this is Paradise, but the air is still, the blue of the heavens deepens, the sun shrinks. It is the quiet before a storm that can never break. The animals draw closer, forming an outer ring around the coffin. The lion lies down with the lamb. Douglas lies unresurrected, an Osiris in street jeans and jacket, a god at once unborn and yet very dead, a corpse in Eden. A white dove hovers in the air above him, shielding his face, his translucent eyelids, from the sun. He is a hero, for he is to be judged.

— I don't know how to judge him,— Mumon finally says in a flat tired voice. — I don't know what to say about him, I don't know what to think about him. I never wanted to be a judge. —

Sister Silvia tosses her head impatiently, sending her curls into waves of golden swirls. — That's just too bad. I don't feel much like being no judge myself. I got work waiting for me, I got clients out on the streets unsatisfied. If we don't judge him, I mean, who the hell will? —

She turns from the fabric of the story, rips free from the tenuous plot that struggles to hold her in place. The others too turn their heads, stare off the page into the eyes of . . .. Who? The Creator? The privacy of thought in the eyes of the reader? Is she after all a judge?

Whom does she accuse? Me? You? Who feels guilty? They stand there, three women and two men, in Paradise, and stare with haunted eyes off the page, into another cross section of time, into another life. Only Douglas remains perfectly dead, feeling no guilt, feeling nothing. It is in their power to bring him back to life, and to whatever life they judge fitting for his soul. And while they wait and worry and try to judge he remains dead.

Butterflies yet spangle the still air, creating fresh air currents with the tremolo of their tiny wings, the sun enlarges and warms, the white dove turns pearly grey, its small head sparkles iridescent, flowers sing their scents in the breeze. A tiger stalks Douglas in his casket with an insolent familiarity, whipping its great black and orange body about in restless circles, although its eyes look mildly out upon the idyllic scene, lobotomized. The lion and lamb gambol and frolic in innocent play, and the lion, pinned to the earth by a delicate hoof upon its massive chest, has eyes more tranquil than the lamb's. In the piney woods shy animals soft and furry chase each other and stare blankly into one another's souls when contact is made.

Introduce then more exotic beasts, parrots with their raucous squawkings, reptiles with diamond patterns emblazoned on their cold skins, Chinese Dragon lizards, a plastic yellowgreen, motionless in the tall grass, monkeys swinging from vines, red-bottomed homunculi with empty greedy eyes, and yet the piney woods is still the piney woods, sweet-smelling, quiet, sun-dappled, mossy, cool, still the meadow is a meadow, lush and clean where flowers bloom anew and sun motes are radiant in the air. There is no violence in Eden! Shogen is a toad indeed, but a jeweled toad, croaking music, Sister Calliope is ancient, withered and sere, but eternal, life blazing anew in the rheum of her eyes. There is no violence in Paradise!

Douglas, how did he die? Relief spread through his blood, bliss wound its way through the convolutions of his brain, pain lay anatomized, anesthetized, dissected, before his sudden understanding, pain lay crippled, dead, very far away, when Douglas died. What is an overdose? How does it feel? How does if feel . . . how does it feel . . .. Or, more simply, what were the physiological symptoms of this death, our dreaded death? How did he die? His lungs froze, paralyzed, and while his body fought for oxygen his soul slipped out on a silver cord, free, eagle-free, high flying free. His face suffused with blood, his skin purpled, and he stood aside with a jesus sweet smile on his face and watched his humanity writhe itself into oblivion. How did he die? Happy, damn and blast it, in paradise, devil take it, that's how this boy did die. There is no violence in Eden! On earth his body suffocated for want of oxygen-liberating life into the bloodstream, but his soul died and stayed alive in Paradise. In a hallway he died a violent death, but there is no violence in . . . there is no requiem for a junkie. There is nothing much to be said. He died happy. He told me so/yeah, says who?

— Do we take into account how he died? — Sister Silvia asks timidly, of her companions, of the butterflies, of air soft as silk and nourishing as mother's milk, but certainly not of the Creator, for no one invokes the Creator in Paradise, not with any sincerity, at any rate. — Do we take into account how he died, or just how he lived? —

Mumon, making an effort to enjoy his rascality, but leaden-voiced just the same, quips, — Any old way you want to judge him, my child. If you think his death important, by all means, count his death. It's his funeral. —

Shogen has regained his equilibrium with very little effort. It's all a matter of concentration. Freshly oiled, his words unfurl perfumed and well chosen. — I think it necessary that we consider his death. After all, is death not the culmination of life? I shall endeavor to prove that his death was a fitting, even predictable climax to the cheap, sleazy, formless life he led.—

Endeavor to prove. You sound like a lawyer. How can you renounce his life? You were his teacher, for god almighty's sake. — Mumon runs a finger along the glass, as if he were caressing the dead man's face.

— And you were my teacher, — Shogen answers, yet you renounce me.—

— That's something else again, — Mumon answers, reluctant to open this question already discussed and left unsettled so many times before. — Besides, I don't really renounce you, you know that. I'm still trying to teach you. I will go on trying to teach you, you ungrateful pup. Oh, that a pupil of mine could turn out so pompous, so smug, so lacking in compassion. —

— What you call compassion is just an excuse for sin, you old reprobate, — Shogen answers. — You go out among the common man in order to be nearer to the stenches of lechery and weakness. I sit at home in the monastery, in rapt contemplation. That is the most valuable lesson I ever learned from my master. But you would go on, you would enter the world, and you have forgotten everything you've ever known. You have cast your own discipline to the four winds. You are a drunkard and a lecher, and I will not follow you there, master.—

Mumon waves his hand at Shogen as if he were waving off a troublesome fly. Yet he does not answer, does not defend himself. Instead, with that same hand he slaps Sister Calliope, who has been dozing on her feet, hard upon the ass. She starts, and his slapping fingers instantly become gentle. He caresses her buttock softly, tickles her a bit, then withdraws his hand. He knows when to stop. — Compassion, — he roars at Shogen. — Compassion! — he roars. Sister Calliope giggles, nudges Mumon in the ribs with her elbow.

— Compassion for Douglas, — Sister Silvia cries. If she were not in Paradise she would weep as well. — Yeah, sure, why not, compassion for Douglas, — Mumon acquiesces. Sister Esta, earth mother to the core, takes up Sister Silvia's battle cry. — Compassion for Douglas! — Wise in her antiquity, Sister Calliope adds her thin quaver,

— Compassion for Douglas. . . .—

The three women improvise wild harmonies, while Mumon supplies a running bass line, — Compassion for Douglas. —

A choir of celestial angels descends from heaven to the earthly garden of delights, caroling a compassion chorus, and leading them is an avenging angel, who lays down his sword and conducts with both hands the music of the spheres. Shogen, his bowels moved, adds his own trained voice, rich and unctuous, wondering all the while at his own unexpected action. — Compassion for Douglas, compassion for Douglas.— And all the beasts of forest and field sang too.

And what of Douglas, undreaming on his bed, glassed in and preserved from Paradise and angel voices and miracles of singing beasts? If the Creator in all majesty were to ask him, Douglas, what he would wish, what then would be his answer? Compassion for Douglas. Douglas, what is it that you wish? All the treasures of the universe are yours for the asking. Douglas from his coffin, from the grave, in all humility, is about to answer, is about to ask of life itself, a favor for eternity. And all he asks, this boy of the streets, is a well-filled uncut bag of heroin every glorious heavenly morning. One well-filled uncut bag of heroin every morning. And God and all the angels wept.

Time closes around him. Space shifts. On a grassy knoll surrounded by a pine forest free of underbrush lay a glass coffin. Dressed in a brown leather jacket and worn jeans and heavy boots, Douglas slept dreamless in the garden, served up rare, under glass. Douglas, mythical and dead, in a corner of paradise, where no insects crawled or flew, and where larks and hummingbirds and yellowbellied sapsuckers hovered in the air or perched, shitless, on tree branches. Birdsong filled the air, rich fugues that anticipated the flute, the violin, the trained soprano castrato. Upon sun-dappled meadows the lion and the lamb lay down together, and cherubs rode plump and naked upon the long-lost supertooth tigers, ecstatic in prehistory. About the glass coffin peacocks strolled, majestic and multi-eyed, their tails permanently spread in sexual potency, viewing paradise blindly from behind, and rending the air with their banshee shrieks. In the distance violet mountains towered. On the other side of the mountains . . .

       . . . is hell.

They convene, they reconvene, they come to judge and are judged. Compassion for Douglas. Let him dispose of his own mortal soul. Douglas chooses nirvana, Douglas overdoses again and again within his own moment of eternity, permanently enlightened, stone high. Back on the streets, locked in a room that is four corners surrounding a street privacy, Doreen without mirror to live with seeks her reflection in a little death, her overdose not yet in her veins, filling a final needle. And others are just shooting junk, and still others are not shooting junk at all, and still others are, alive and dead, still others. . . .

And can I intrude upon all this, into these streets, this garden? If they look out from these printed pages can I look in? If their eyes meet mine dare my eyes meet theirs? Compassion for Douglas. If I can penetrate this wall of print to meet his eyes, what would I see?

Douglas is dead. I think he was a pretty sexy looking cat. I would like to have touched him, to have placed an arm upon the stiffness of his jacket, the softness of the worn fabric of his jeans encasing his lean thighs. I know his clothing. Of the flesh and blood that is his body, of his body . . . what do I know? I would like to touch him, touch his clothing, touch his body, touch his immortal soul. But he has escaped from me. The wall between us is denser than my will. I think Douglas is a pretty sexy cat. But he is so private, so dead, and he was so alive, that I cannot intrude upon him.

Douglas in a garden. A garden of earthly delights.

THE SOUND OF WOMEN'S VOICES

The women spent the afternoon drinking Ripple and talking about their abortions. Early in the day a fine snow began to fall, and as the weather hovered at the freezing point, sometimes warming, sometimes cooling, the snow mixed with rain and hail, so that the streets quickly turned slushy. The wind blew, violent and erratic, shaking the fragile windows, and a little pile of dirty snow sifted in upon the windowsill, where it was long in melting. Slightly after one Doreen stuffed rags along the perimeter of the window, and pulled the shade down against the sunless gloom. The electric lights had been burning all day. With the view of the grey afternoon so suddenly cut off, the room seemed even smokier, more cluttered. Doreen emptied the ashtrays, and stood staring into the garbage bag, her left hand twitching in a gesture of apology. The room was cheerless, the women depressed, and there was nothing much she could do about it.

Desiree grunted, shifted her weight on the bed. The bedsprings echoed her groans. "Break out the rest of the juice, honey. If your landlord won't send no heat, we just gonna provide our own." Her voice was loud, rich, warm. On the floor her youngest daughter, not yet school age, looked up from her diligent application of a purplish pink lipstick to a four day old newspaper, and smiled vaguely. She liked the vibrato of her mother's voice. Her mother drained the dregs of wine from her glass, and grinned back, winking. Gratified, her daughter returned to her drawing. Doreen, relieved, opened another bottle and refilled glasses. The women brightened perceptibly, and the room seemed cozy, sheltered, warm. Desiree waved her glass at her daughter and at her infant son sleeping on an improvised cradle of folded towels underneath the table where no one would stumble across him.

"Yeah, I had the two more and I guess I'll keep having them. That A.B. was too bad. That was about the closest I ever come to dying. I lay there in that hospital bed and I prayed. I said Lord, if this is a sign, then give me one more chance. You just let me keep on living to take care of the kids I already got, and I will have more as you send them to me. I know I done wrong, dear Jesus. Let me live and I will have more babies to bring up good Christians to honor your name. That's exactly the way I prayed it, every word. And I lived. That's how I knew it was a sign, because I prayed and I lived. And as long as I got a good man who can keep me awake at night, I'm going to keep on having children."

"You're lucky you can keep on having children," Mona said softly. "I had a cousin, she had an abortion and they had to take her whole insides out. Eighteen and they took her whole insides out. She's never gonna have kids. And she's like an old lady. Her cunt's all dried up. She gotta grease up whenever she makes it. I bet she dies young. Women they take their insides out, they die young."

Mona leapt into a moody silence, her eyes hard and far away. The other women ignored her. They knew that when women talk about such things, bad thoughts rise unbidden and have to be dealt with in silence, alone. During the course of the afternoon, each one of them would have, in turn, her own need for silence, and the others would discreetly ignore the retreat. Desiree laughed, her voice blanketing the hard quiet edge that Mona had carved in the soft warmth of the room. Desiree was the oldest of the women, the oldest, the fattest, the loudest, the happiest, and they all respected her, even as they sneered at her age, her square broad hips, her ignorance, her heavily overlaid cosmetics fashionable when she was still in high school.

"Yeah, I wish that had happened to me. I wish they had taken my insides out. Hell, I got all the use I'll ever want out of them. That way I coulda had my cake and eaten it too. The Lord God woulda letted me live just the same, and I woulda given him all the kids he was gonna give me, which woulda been an even none, cause I wouldn't a had any place to put them, what with my little kangaroo pouch cut out. But God is too foxy for me. He almost killed me with that A.B. I got, and then he let me live and left my insides in a far better state of health than they had any right to be in." She sipped her wine thoughtfully, her eyes alive and starry bright with an eager appreciation of God's sense of justice, God's sense of humor. Doreen, less sensitive to God's mischievous streak, for she had borne no children, was worried. "Why don't you use a diaphragm or something. That way you wouldn't get caught all the time. It's not the same thing as having an abortion."

"Sure it is," Desiree answered, her voice confident. She had answered this question before, in bed, often, to her husband's querulous, insistent pestering. "I promised God to have babies he sent me. Now God has only one way of sending babies, and I don't aim to trick him, and I won't let any man of mine trick him either, because God is smarter than people, and if you decide to trick him, well, he's just gonna trick you twice as hard. He let me live, see, and he can just as easy say, well, you tricked me, now I'm gonna trick you, don't look now but you're dead. The way I figure it is, if I have the babies I promised him, then he'll put me through the change early. That's what he'll do. Shit, it came on when I was just turned nine, that's early all right. So I figure the change will come early too."

Her baby woke up, and wailed his dislike of sleeping under a table, where the draft from the window, rags or no rags, had stiffened his neck and cramped his legs. Sylvia, who had been sitting quietly by the table, too shy to talk because she had never been pregnant, let alone had such mysterious things as babies or abortions, knelt and picked up the crying boy, glad of the opportunity to demonstrate her as yet unproven femininity. She cradled him to her breast, trembling at the brink of fantasy, remembering a madonna blue shawl she had seen in a store window, deciding that she would buy it after all as the baby sucked wetly at the bunched up Orlon of her sweater covering her milkless breast.

"Hand over that screaming brat, honey," Desiree said, unbuttoning her blouse. Her breast, heavy and drooping, was swollen and firm at the aureole, and her nipples, enormous and purple, stood erect, a bluish drop of milk forming, then running over into a deep crease between layers of rubbery belly. "You may be younger and firmer and prettier than me, Sylvia, and my old man would sooner choose you to love than me, but my son here, he wants only one thing from a woman, and you ain't got it, honey. This little cat is faithful to the death." She placed the baby to her breast, and he turned, his eyes screwed shut, his face darkening ecstatically, and drew nipple and aureole into his pursed lips. His mouth pumped furiously, his hands, balled into tight fists, slid up along the puckered skin of her breasts. His first hunger abated, he settled into a steady sucking rhythm, his fists stroking the velvety skin in time to his gulps. Mona looked away, disgusted. "Why don't you give him a bottle? No one does that any more."

Desiree leaned further back on the bed, stroked her baby with her empty hand. "Some folk do."

"Yeah, some do, but there ain't no reason to any more."

"I got the best reason in the world, Mona, considering my promise I made. I don't get my period so long as I let him suck, and I don't get pregnant either. He keeps me safe the natural way, and I love him for it. I'm gonna let him suck until he's two years old. I'm not having no more babies till he's big enough to take care of himself, wipe his own ass."

Mona nodded her head, still keeping her eyes averted from Desiree's hanging breast, from the baby's suction-tensed face. She stood abruptly, awkwardly, and poured herself another glass of wine. She drained the glass, then poured another. She returned to her chair, found herself straining her neck to avoid catching glimpses of the purpled nipple, the transported infant. She changed her seat, complaining of the cold.

Desiree swung the baby over her shoulder, patting it on the back. She kept her blouse unbuttoned. Her breast was flabby, drained, the nipple lay large, dark, and flat. Although Mona could not see it, she could not help thinking of it. She imagined, against her will, herself

sucking at that breast. She imagined the dark, squirming baby sucking at her own pale nipple, her nipple pale and large and equally
flattened and distended. She shuddered, grew embarrassed, as if the
rest of the women had read her thought, and she rubbed her hands
against her upper arms, her arms crossed over her soft, freckled
bosom hidden beneath a shaggy brown sweater. She rubbed hard, in
an exaggerated manner, and complained, this time loudly, of the
cold. "It's never gonna get warm again. It's gonna stay winter forever, I could swear it. God, how I hate the cold."

"Finish up your wine," Desiree coaxed. "That wine will warm you
up. That wine would warm the soul of an Eskimo sitting on top of
the North Pole." She shoved her breast back into the brassiere cup,
buttoned her blouse, and swung the infant down her shoulder and
onto her knees. Her daughter stood by her side. The little girl
reached out a hand and poked at her mother's chest. Desiree slapped
the hand away. "Don't you go touching that. That ain't nice." The
little girl hunched up, stuck a thumb in her mouth, and kept her eyes
fixed on her mother's blouse, on the pearly button that seemed as if
it would slip any moment from the button hole, revealing the stitch-
ing of the brassiere cup emphasizing the spongy purple nipple.
"That child. She knows enough not to come near me when I'm nursing that there baby or I'd break her head for her. But the minute I'm
done with the baby she's all over me, sneaking in a poke when I'm
not looking. What's the matter with you? That don't belong to you.
That's the baby's. Keep your hands offa me." Silvia clapped her
hands. The little girl turned around and stared at the clapping
woman, at her piled up blonde hair and woolly white dress. The
pretty, young woman beckoned, both hands inviting the child
towards her. The child smiled. "And take that thumb outa your
mouth. You ain't no baby." Desiree slapped the child's hand down.
"You gonna get buck teeth and look like a sick squirrel if you keep
up that there habit." The little girl ran across the room and climbed
up on Silvia's lap. Silvia took a suck of the little girl's thumb.
"Mmm. Tastes yummy. What's your name?"

"Aimee. It means love in French."

"Pretty. My name's Silvia."

"I know that. What does your name mean?"

"I don't know. We can make up what it means. What do you think it should mean?"

"It should mean love too."

"Okay. But not in French. In Martian. It means love in Martian. Martian is my favorite language."

Aimee nestled against Silvia. Surreptitiously she stroked the furry Orlon sweater, the small hard swelling that shaped the sweater. Silvia didn't seem to notice at all.
"That child ain't bothering you, is she?" Desiree looked sharply at them from across the room.

"No, she ain't bothering me."

"That's good. Don't bother the lady now. She ain't used to kids."

In the hush that followed, the wind's voice sounded shrill, anguished, a howl from the outside, a begging to come in, into the bright, the light, the warm, where Ripple flowed like water and women's voices sounded sweet and soothing. The glass panes rattled in the sashes, and the shade snapped as the air current tortured its still form. "It must be twenty after," Doreen said, with a nervous giggle. "An angel must be flying over us. That's why we're all so quiet. It's twenty after. It must be."

Footsteps pounded hollowly up the stairs. A rapid knocking was heard at the door. The women started, then they all leaned back, retaining their alertness, as Mona rose and answered the knock at the door. She stood at the open door, peering out uncertainly into the dark of the hallway. The landlord had not yet replaced the blown-out light bulb at the top of the landing. "Oh, it's you." Her tone was noncommittal. She stepped aside as another young woman strode into the room, her stiletto heels clicking, pocking the linoleum with miniscule heel marks. Snow frosted the black fur of her collar, sil-vered her majestic reddish-brown Afro-styled hair. Gloria slid out of her coat, handed it to Mona with imperious disdain. "What you all drinking? Ripple? Talk about low. Mona honey, pour me a glass, I'm frozen." Mona dropped the coat onto a chair, gritted her teeth, and slopped some wine into the glass she had been drinking from. She held the glass out at full arm's length. Gloria fluffed her hair, spraying moisture into the air, and took the proffered glass. "Ripple in a jelly glass. Very cute. What you been talking about, all you dirty girls?"

"Abortions," Aimee piped up brightly.

"Ooh, abortions, isn't that sweet. Which one had the most abor-tions?"

"I guess I did," Doreen said. "I had three."

"Well, meet the new champ," Gloria crowed. "I had five. I just been shopping. I'm having it delivered. I knew I'd find someone here. God, I hate this weather. It's so depressing out there. Who had the bloodiest one?"

"Desiree, I guess. She almost died. Was in the hospital for a week." Doreen watched with a non-condemning curiosity to see what Gloria's response would be. Gloria rattled on, non-responsive, care-fully controlling the modulation of her voice, striving for effect, in an effort to captivate, to dazzle, the roomful of stolid drinkers. Nothing important could ever have happened to Desiree. She was too old, too fat, too common to have any role in life's drama than that of an avid listener to Gloria's accounts of adventure. Gloria herself was very impressed with the romance that was her life. "Yeah, I bet I had the cleanest abortion ever. The most expensive, too. Good thing I wasn't the one paying for it. If that there man woulda had a kid, that kid woulda got the best of everything. Swimming pools, nursemaids, ponies, summer camp in some European country . . . that man had money."

"Maybe he did have kids who really did get all that. Maybe he was a married man. Honey." Mona spoke into her glass, into purple bubbles breaking on the surface that somehow reminded her, fascinated her, in their resemblance to spit, of . . .. She sipped at the purple spit, trying to catch and hold a purple bubble on her tongue. Wine trickled over her chin and spotted her sweater.

Gloria looked at her, shocked. She didn't realize that Mona was such a suspicious type. Catty, at that. She shrugged. "He wasn't the marrying type. He's like me. Anyway, if I woulda had a kid I bet he woulda got it the world on a silver platter. But I don't want to bother having kids. Not yet. I wanna hold onto my figure. It's one thing I really have going for me. Anyway, so I figured why not give that little kid the best abortion money could buy. After all, his daddy was a rich man. What a set-up that deal was, like in a spy movie. I swear to Christ."

"You shouldn't swear by God," Aimee said primly, looking to her mother for approval. Desiree flashed a warm, gap-toothed smile at her daughter, then pursed her lips and frowned at Gloria. Gloria was lost in dreamy reminiscence, near ecstatic reliving of a delightful, thrilling highlight of womanly triumph and danger. "Dig it. I took a train to Philadelphia, and was met at the station by a Cadillac. I was wearing an orchid on my suit so the driver would recognize me. From there we drove to this luncheonette a few blocks away, and another car, a Mercury, if I remember right, picked me up there. And then we drove from Philly all the way to Washington, D.C. And that whole drive I'm so scared I'm getting the shits, I'm thinking this is some set-up, they could be kidnapping me and no one would even know I was gone or where I was going, except for this one rich cat and who knows where that man got his money from, maybe by shanghaiing and selling foxy broads, you understand what I mean? So there we was riding and riding and me getting nervous, you know, more and more nervouser, and then we come into Washington, we drive into this lonely section of Washington, the outskirts of town kinda, and he pulls up at a corner and says get out. I'm real glad to get out of that car, you best believe it, so I get out. He's kind of tough-looking, Italian-like, you understand me? No offense meant, if any of you girls is part Italian. We all sisters, sisters under the skin." Gloria took a deep breath, and looked up bright-eyed, as if daring anyone who was the least bit Italian to get offended.

Doreen, whose father had leavened her pale Irish beauty with a hefty flavoring of Italian blood, looked modestly at the floor, unoffended. She firmly believed that Italian men were tough-looking. Her father certainly had been.

Mona sulked in a corner, wishing she were Italian, unable to defend in any other way her mounting outrage. A narrow incantation began in her brain, "Come on, slut, say something about the Irish, come on, you nigger bitch." As the prayer repeated faster and faster, boiling in her throat, tickling her tongue, she looked guiltily at Desiree and Aimee, suddenly terrified that they might read her thoughts. She didn't have anything against Negroes, black people, she silently corrected herself, just snotty high-class acting nigger bitches like Gloria. Think they got something special down between their legs. Hell, it was just plain old cunt, charred by the hand of God, but no better than good old white pussy. She steadily belted wine and stared at the nut-gold shimmer of Gloria's stockinged legs crossing and uncrossing for emphasis, for punctuation, as she talked.

"This section of Washington wasn't no slum, y'understand. It was all nice houses, private houses, like a suburb. Only it was getting dark, and there wasn't a store for blocks, just all these houses, and it was all deserted. All them straight people eating din-din with their stupid families. So the Italian cat says wait here, and I stood on that street corner watching it get darker, and in less than five minutes another car pulls up from around the corner, it musta been parked there all the time, waiting on me, a Cadillac again this time. Real style. And this time the driver is a brother, you know, it's this young black cat that I can talk to, real nice looking too, so I told him all I was thinking about driving with that Mafia ape. How I thought I was being kidnapped and sent to Buenos Aires or some place, where I'd be forced to make it with all these Spanish cats and Chinks and everything. I can hack it with Spanish cats, they're cool, but Chinks really give me the creeps. And they'd make me work my ass off Saturday night and then make me go to Mass on Sunday, Catholics is like that, and I was born a Baptist, though I don't believe in any of that shit no more."

Desiree stirred restively, and Gloria quickly added, "But I respect it. I respect all of it, even the Catholics. Except for the Jews. Ain't no Jews here, though, is there?" Gloria laughed, quick and crisp, with a little shake of her head and a characteristic motion, half shiver, half shimmy, to her shoulders. "So this cat tells me not to worry, and soon we are jiving and I'm not so scared. Then he asks me very polite would I put on this blindfold, dig it, and I let him put it on and we drive some more and when we finally stop he takes off the blindfold and we are in a garage and we walk up some stairs and through this door to where there's a desk where there's this nurse and we're in some kind of hospital and the doctor came and took me through the halls of this little hospital, only it's nothing but an abortion hospital, but they have some kind of cover that it's a private rest home for chicks with nervous breakdowns, and I had a regular operation with ether and nurses with those little white masks on, and they keep you overnight with breakfast in the morning in case something should go wrong."

Gloria stopped, confused, aware that something had gone wrong with her story. The faces she turned to were all silent, stony, remote.

Aimee was turned expectantly to her, however, her thumb in her mouth, sleep-heavy eyes closing, then widening again to take in once more the fairytale-like elegance, the bold crown of red-tinted hair, the gleaming stockings, the soft, clinging mauve dress. "Look at that child listening. Well, little kids gotta learn, don't they? Specially a little girl. They gotta learn to take care of themselves. Ooh, ooh, what my mama didn't tell me. I had to learn it all the hard way. I was a very sheltered child. Real spoiled. I always got everything I wanted. My mama was a church-going woman."

"So was mine," Doreen said timidly, suddenly sorry for Gloria, sensing the spasm of loneliness that had just come over the so self-confident girl.

"That a fact?" Gloria answered, pleased, paying gracious attention to Doreen, whom she usually dismissed as mousy.

"Yeah, my mother and Mona's too. And Desiree's mother too, I bet." Doreen waited for someone to make a connection, to find the point, to applaud the coincidences and direct them toward conclusion.

"My mother too," shrilled Aimee. The point seemed lost, and Gloria and Doreen groped towards understanding with eyes soft and panicky as a doe's. Silvia, crestfallen, said sadly, "My mother wouldn't set foot in a church for the love of God or money." She sat curled in upon herself, ashamed, hiding the silvery sexuality of her teenaged body, a fallen female, her womb never stretched by an embryonic struggle towards humanhood, never violated by needle, knife, or suction cup, the womb that she herself had sprung from locked within a body that never went to church or wore a flowered hat on Sundays. Nubile and warm-blooded, dressed in a white crocheted thigh-high skirt and brown sweater, her white-blonde hair artfully tousled, she curled inward toward her own emptiness of experience, lamb-like, highly sexually charged and knowledgeable, innocent of womanliness, a whorish kitten. "My

29

mother was a real wild one. Ooh, she was bad." She smiled, a grace note of pride.

"Children should change a woman," Desiree mused, scratching between her breasts. Though the room was chilly her bulk warmed itself, and in her cleavage and between her thighs sweat always puddled, so that she was usually mildly tormented by rashes. "I don't care how bad she was, how wild, how mean, well, that's just being young. Hell, I once weighed no more than a hundred and five pounds, and was a handful of meanness. But children should change a woman." She nodded to herself with satisfaction; she knew what a woman should be.

"Some women, they never change, they don't wanna change, they don't change. Some women just like to stay young. Having a kid didn't change me, and it ain't never gonna ever. I'm never gonna change. I'm hard, I'm mean, and I'm young and I like it that way."

Mona swayed, drunk, truculent, to the center of the room, held her ground like a maddened bull, red-eyed, nostrils flaring. Doreen moved toward her, gripped with iron hands Mona's shoulders, whispering "Ssshhh" with unaccustomed ferocity into Mona's ear. Mona shook her off, took a step forward, tottered, then shook her head, trying to clear the rosy mist. "Shee-it, what we need is more wine. I'm going out for more wine." She slipped into her raincoat and headed out the door. They listened to her clattering down the stairs, bedroom slippers flopping in erratic arrhythmic shocks of sound. She didn't fall. They heard the front door slam closed five flights down. Doreen rushed to the window and watched Mona negotiate crossing the street. Doreen's hand flew to her mouth, and she bit down on her clenched knuckles. She turned to the room, to the other women, to her sisters, to plead for help, and was confronted by three placid impassive faces. She opened her palms toward them, unable to find words to express her need, Mona's needs. The gesture, poignant but weak, drew no sympathy.

"Why does that broad drink so goddamn much?" Doreen finally said, breaking the flinty silence. "She is nasty when she drinks. And it seems she is always drinking nowadays."

"Yeah, I used to see her around a while back, before her kid disappeared in that weird way, she used to be a real quiet one. Aida Gomez told me she was a junkie, but she looks like a plain old lush to me," Gloria said, arching her eyebrows in appreciation of her probing subtlety.

"She was a junkie," Doreen admitted tonelessly. "She stopped using junk since her kid died – disappeared, I mean." She shivered. "We don't really know if it's dead, do we?" She stared broodingly at Aimee. The child was the same age as Mona's child had been when she died – or disappeared, rather. "She'll be a junkie again. There's nothing much else she can be. She don't like to drink."

"Something was wrong with her kid, wasn't there?" Desiree said slowly. "I mean, it seems like the kid wasn't right in the head, you know what I mean? That kid was only half there." She tapped her forehead with her index finger, then twirled the finger around in little circles. "The kid was kinda slow."

"She was not!" Doreen flared. "She was a real smart kid!"

"She was still drinking from a bottle and she was almost four years old," Desiree said firmly, as if that were that. "I know I didn't want Aimee playing with her. She was peculiar."

"Her mother sure is peculiar, at any rate," Gloria added. Silvia giggled, and the three women began to roar with laughter, while Doreen watched in helpless disbelief, her eyes swimming with voluptuous tears.

"I think you all really got Mona upset, talking about abortions the way you did. I mean you was talking about kids you coulda had but didn't want, and here she is her kid gone, a kid she wants and can't have. I mean none of us really thought about how she felt. Jesus, Gloria, you talked about your abortion like it was a lot of fun." Doreen rubbed her eyes with her knuckles in a little girl way, standing frail and skinny before the other three fleshy earthy women. She vacillated between accusation and her customary apologetic style, too ludicrous to achieve pure pathos, the red blotches on her shapeless, stick-like legs, the pinkness of her eyelids, the collapsed cupping of a too-big brassiere about her drooping miniscule breasts destroying the tragic effect that her compassion for Mona should have wrought. Her nose was running, and she swiped at it with that same childlike gesture that she used when drying her teary eyes or pushing back her lank hair from her forehead.

"You make it sound like Mona is the only one who ever suffered, like I never suffered at all," Gloria cried petulantly. "When I had that shitty abortion you think I didn't feel something? When I awoke the doctor was standing over me grinning, waving a tiny mess of blood around in a plastic bag. All out, babe, he said, and then I saw that that was my baby he was waving around in that plastic bag. You're a virgin again, he said, and then he tossed the goddamn thing right into this garbage can over in a corner. You know, sometimes I still dream about it, and the worst part of the dream is that awful thud the bag made falling into that empty garbage can. Thunk, it sounded like. Thunk. But I don't go around making a big deal about my sufferings, I don't put my thing on other people. I try to be light, you know, I have this optimistic philosophy on life. Mona's too heavy, girl, she is a drag-ass bitch if you want my opinion. I wouldn't be surprised if she sold her kid on the black market for someone to adopt because she was strung out and needed money for dope."

Gloria, vindicated, triumphant, stood up, then suddenly swept Aimee into her arms and hugged her tight, lavishing kisses on the child's head. Aimee drank in Gloria's perfume, delighted. "I just wish I had a baby. All I've ever had is abortions. But I'm not gonna have a kid until I can afford it. My kid's gonna get the best of every-thing. I don't know why women like Mona should be allowed to have kids. It's a disgrace. Women like that should be sterilized, I swear to God."

Aimee, startled by Gloria's vehemence, half smothered by Gloria's tightening embrace, squirmed loose. Doreen, distracted, was gazing out the window, shaking her fingers in a whirlwind flurry, agitated to the point of shrillness. "Oh God, she's coming back. Look at how she's crossing the street. Why does she go out like that? She'll catch pneumonia. It's freezing out there, the street's all icy. She'll slip and break her neck in those stupid slippers."

"Don't worry about her, she can't feel a thing, she's so tanked up," Sylvia said, coming to stand with Doreen at the window. Her voice held a tart edge to it, but her eyes were wide and deep and open. "Why can't you ask them to leave," she added in a low voice, lay-ing her hand lightly on Doreen's, then squeezing into immobility the nervously fluttering fingers. "I'll stay on a bit if you want some help calming her down, or putting her to bed. My mother used to drink just like that, get all mean like. I've got experience handling this kind of thing."
Silvia's voice was this time soothing, almost hypnotic, but her eyes glittered overly wise, so lupine, in her child's face. Doreen was overwhelmed by bewilderment, by a sense of her own weakness. She felt like nobody at all. "Yes. Yes, that's a good idea."

"Tell them to leave," Silvia urged.
"Maybe you all better leave before she gets back up here. She's got more wine and she's gonna get screaming mad. I know her." Doreen's voice, wispy, slightly hoarse, seemed to drown in the heavy unforgiving righteousness she was meeting in Desiree and Gloria.

"Mommy, let's go home," Aimee whimpered, frightened, not so much of Mona but of Doreen's terrible fear, her ineffectual distress.

"That's a good idea," Desiree said, "because when I'm screamed at, I scream back, and that pale little mick ain't no match for me, drunk or sober."

"I got my shopping being delivered," Gloria remembered, reaching for her coat. As she drew it on she smiled condescendingly at Doreen. "It sure was good seeing you, honey. We'll get together again real soon, in better circumstances, I hope. I don't know why you put up with Mona. It's my opinion that that child needs a little vacation on the funny farm. She's really coming to pieces."

The door downstairs slammed, hard. Faint footsteps could be heard, growing louder. They had a defiant ring to them. "I'll dress the kids downstairs. I ain't gonna hang around wrapping them up under her sour eye. Well, it's just a step over to where we live. Maybe we'll just run over the way we are." Desiree hurriedly shoved her hastily gathered array of coats into Gloria's arms, and wrapped her infant son up in a heavy quilted blanket of a mild sky blue. His name, Dwight Evan, was embroidered in white along the border. She hustled Aimee along, yanking a little too hard on the child's arm in her haste, and Aimee began to scream, more with fatigue than with pain. "I'll see you girls again real soon. Why don't you all drop in on me, huh? Only leave that crazy woman at home when you do." She turned to go out the door, and nearly collided with Mona, who stood there, dazed, her nose and cheeks reddened with cold and drink.

Mona stared hungrily, stupidly, at Aimee, stretched out a hand as if to caress her, then drew it hurriedly back, clutching at her bag full of Ripple as she felt it start to slip. Silvia hurried over and took the bag from her, while Doreen took her arm and tried to guide her towards the bed. Mona pulled away, to stare at the figure of the small girl dragged out the door by her mother. "Who's that?" Mona slurred. "Who's that kid?"

"That's Aimee," Silvia answered, putting the bag of wine bottles on the table by the window. The door was slammed shut, and Mona continued to gaze in the direction of the departing child while Silvia deftly opened a bottle and poured out three glasses of wine.

"I don't know no Aimee. Anyway, she ain't my kid, is she?" Mona flopped heavily onto the bed, seemed about to lie down, but the sanguineous gleam of the filled glasses caught her eye and she sprang towards them. She took two long gulps, then returned to the bed, keeping the glass in precarious balance as she settled herself delicately into a position compatible with drinking.

"Bring me that bottle," she commanded, and though Doreen hesitated Sylvia brought the bottle promptly. "Who the hell are you?" Mona asked as she tucked the bottle safely between her ankles, where she could feel it, feel its chill comfort.

"I'm Sylvia," Silvia replied with a direct simplicity, disarming save for the strange bitter glow in her eyes.

"Don't know you," Mona dismissed her.

"Yes you do. Ma."

Doreen started. Somewhat tipsy herself, she was uncertain if she had heard correctly. The girl looked so young, so innocent. She couldn't have said Ma. She couldn't. But Mona had heard it too.

"I ain't your fucking pus-assed mother," she snarled.

"Yes you are. You're my mother. You are. You are." Silvia's voice was perfectly a child's, with the pure high timbre of a child. The harshly feeble 60 watt bulb threw heavy shadows on her face, yet her face too, distorted by one ghastly light, bore a fantastical resemblance to Karen's, the missing three year old child that both Mona and Doreen knew was dead. Before Doreen or Mona could react, she continued in her normal voice, "You really do remind me a lot of my mother. She used to drink the same way you do. But you're not really a lush at all, not the way she was. This is just a freaky thing with you. You're really a junkie, both of you are really junkies. I can tell. My sister Calliope taught me how to read faces. She's a very wise old woman, perhaps the wisest in the world. She's really my true mother. Mothers and sisters and friends. All women are sisters, aren't they?"

Sylvia began to pace, and Doreen and Mona followed her metronomic path, stupefied by wine, by the radiant halo of her hair, the peripatetic charm she was weaving, the strange pentagramic pattern of movement. "I never had a mother, not a real one. Like Topsy, I was made, not born. Found under a cabbage leaf. But I can call you Ma, can't I? I need to. Ma. Ma. Mama." Her voice took on again the true ring of childhood, but this time growing plaintive, frightened. Mona flung up her hand before her face, as if warding off evil spirits, and her wine sloshed over her, staining her already soiled clothes, the grimy sheet of the bed. "It looks like blood," Sylvia quavered, then laughed, brittle, needle-like.

"Go away," Mona growled.

"Yes, I have to. Douglas and Freddie are on their way up here, and I don't want to see them. Douglas is bringing home a bottle of wine, Doreen, as a surprise. He wants to cheer you up, to encourage you, because you're clean, you're not using junk any more . . . at least for awhile."

"How do you know that?" Doreen whimpered. "How do you know Douglas? You never met Douglas."

"Oh, but I did, years ago. He hates me. Tell him that Sister Silvia was here. I want him to know that his fate has been around, that he's not free. Tell me, do you think that Douglas is Jesus Christ?"

Doreen sat heavily into the straight-backed chair near the window and laid her head on the table. Her stomach heaved, and she was afraid she was going to be sick, but the feeling passed, leaving only a cold numbness at the pit of her stomach. That Douglas was Jesus Christ, was God himself, was her favorite, most hidden, most shameful fantasy.

"And you are Mary Magdalene, aren't you, playing the whore to feed his habit. Saint Junkie Christ, Magdalene's pimp. What a mess you Catholics make of things when you lose your faith. You make a new religion out of your weaknesses. Tell Douglas that his fate was here and is still around. He's gonna have to crucify himself for me to believe he's really God's own son. Tell him that for me, huh? Tell him Sister Sylvia said hello. Hey Doreen, about that friend of yours drinking blood over there in the corner of her own weird perversion of the Eucharist, get her back on junk. She loses her identity when she makes out she's a lush. But you ought to know what it's like to lose your identity, right, Douglas's girl friend? Who are you, shadow? Who are you, shadow under his blazing sun? You have sinned, mavourneen, you have forgotten that a shadow is not created by the sun alone, but by an object standing in the sun's radiant glow."

Speechless, Doreen looked up at the pretty lamb-like blonde, hearing in her voice the croak, the characteristic gravel of Douglas's speaking voice. The girl's face looked hideous, like the face of an ancient, sexless mummy. Then Silvia laughed, and Mona was sobbing desperately, and Silvia was saying in her ordinary brash, banal way, "Oh wow, we really got ourselves dead drunk. I'm not used to this. Can you manage without me, hon? She's crying, but she seems pretty quiet. Not mean at all. Take care, Doreen. I'll come up tomorrow to see how things are going, if I don't have too bad a hangover. I gotta go home and get some sleep. I feel half dead."

She was out the door, and Doreen wondered whether Sylvia had been wearing a coat, and where she lived, and couldn't remember anything about her, or where she met her, or even what she looked like. "I wonder if Douglas really knows her," Doreen sighed, injured. "Calling me a whore. Sure I'm a whore, but she's the worst little tramp I've ever seen. She'd do it with anybody, anything, animals even. I heard she made a couple of movies with another woman, an old man, and a Doberman Pinscher. A dog, for Chrissakes. And she does it because she likes it. She don't even need the money, she don't use junk or anything. I hope Douglas comes home soon, I really do, oh, I really do."

Mona looked up, her tear-streaked face contorted into an unrecognizable expression, a compound of the most agonizing of human emotions, with hate and terror predominating. "Where is my baby," she wailed. "What did Freddie do with my baby?"

Doreen staggered across the room, knelt besides Mona, clumsily embraced her, kissing her roughened lips, chewed bloody during her fit of crying. She locked her arms around her, rocked her back and forth, their tears mingling together, Doreen making hushing sounds as Mona muffled inarticulate cries, the two of them sharing the taste of blood, mouth to mouth. It was thus that Freddie and Douglas found them when they opened the door and jauntily breezed in, Freddie with the evening newspapers, damp and musty smelling from the snow and rain, and Douglas with a bottle of wine under his arm. "Surprise!" they caroled out, then stopped dead in their tracks, as the sight of the two drunken, dirty, disheveled women kissing and crying and pawing at each other's hair met their eyes.

"Christ, wouldn't you know it," Freddie yelped in disgust. "A pair of fucking lesbians. Oh Jesus."

"Shut up!" howled Mona, "Shut up, shut up, shut up, you never gave birth to a baby, you never had your insides tortured by an abortion, you don't know a fucking thing, you slob, you ignorant slob, you never had a baby, shut up, shut up, shut up!"

Freddie, free with his hands and intolerant of drunks, particularly drunken women, raised his fists, then put them down again, his eyes gentling. He turned his back on them and rubbed thoughtfully, ruefully, at an old scar that ran across the left side of his face, from cheekbone to nostril. Douglas was smiling, not gently at all.

"Yeah, shut up," Doreen piped thinly, "you never had an abortion, you dirty sons a bitches." Douglas laughed, hugged her roughly, then turned away, and, like Freddie, rubbed his face meditatively. "You girls been having a little party?" he asked.

"What's a party?" Mona yelled. I never had no party, I don't know what no party feels like. Oh it's okay for you, for men life is nothing but one big poison party, but for women it's different."

"Yeah," shrilled Doreen, "for women it's different."

"What party?" Mona wept, "What fucking party? We was just kissing each other, that's all. We was just kissing, not for sex, not because it felt good, but because we was women, and we don't know party. Party, party, party. Fuck you."

Doreen sank weakly onto the floor. "Yeah, fuck you."

Douglas sat next to her, put his hand on the nape of her neck. Doreen melted against him, giggling, frowning, giggling. "Silvia says hello. Sister Silvia says hello." She did not see his face grow pale, nor his eyes grow cold as jade, but she felt his arm stiffen. "What's a matter, you don't like old Silvia, old White Goddess Queen of the Jungle Silvia? I don't like her either. She says she hates you. She says she's your fate and she hates you. What's that mean?"

"What does it mean when a man's fate hates him?" Douglas gravely replied, talking to the child within her,

"Pretty bad news, huh?" Doreen kept giggling, her head lolling on his shoulder, dribble wetting his breast as she talked against him, into the crisp cool of his shirt through his unzipped jacket. She clutched the heavy leather, impressed by its weight, its solidarity.

"You're real, huh?" she begged. "But Sister Sylvia, she's ain't real."

"No, she ain't real," Douglas solemnly agreed. He maintained his composure, but his heart was thumping heavily, and he found it difficult to breathe. "Sister Sylvia is just an hallucination of mine, an hallucination I had when I was a crazy young punk running around trying to kill people. She was just a dream. I dreamed her."

"I dreamed her too," Doreen said. "She said I was just your shadow, so I must dream shadows of your dreams. That must be it, huh?"

Douglas almost gagged. "Yes. Yes, Doreen, Doreen mavourneen." He held her tight, pulling her into himself. "So my fate is still around, my dream is still hanging around. Well well well, what do you think of that?" Douglas and Doreen held each other, two trembling animals hulking on the floor.

"Bastards!" Mona suddenly shouted. "Rotten no good filthy bastards, with those ridiculous pieces of fish bait dangling between your legs. Men, you're not people, you're half a person, you fucking animal, Freddie, you don't have any insides, you can't have babies, what did you do with my baby?" And then she was throwing things, smashing glasses, spraying Douglas and Doreen with wine dregs and glass splinters, and they crouched on the floor, while Freddie balled and unballed his hands, unable to act.

Mona was now screaming incoherently, great torrents of animal sounds, her hands clutching her womb, ripping at her clothing, scrabbling to enter, to tear out her insides, and as she vomited wordless sounds of rage she was also vomiting wine, vomiting onto the floor, stumbling up and down the length of the room, vomiting promiscuously upon everything, upon Douglas's legs, upon her own feet in their snow-soaked bedroom slippers, upon Freddie's hands as they raised gently to her face, and then he was holding her, keeping her firmly in one place, and she puked until she was empty, and she continued to puke, great dry wrenching movements of her stomach, until she was screaming with pain, and Freddie was stroking back her vomit-streaked hair, murmuring brokenly I love you I love you I love you over and over again. When she caught her breath and stood swaying, empty-bellied but with a raging heart, he stripped the bed of its dirty sheet, laid her down upon it, and began to mop up the mess.

"You bastard!" she cried out, and he answered quietly, "I love you, I love you baby," and as he humbly knelt and swabbed the floor she spat into his hair and sneered, "You bastard, don't think I would do the same for you. If it was you I'd rub your nose in it, pig," and he mildly replied, this little dark scarred man who had killed people, "But I love you."

And Mona laughed and laughed and laughed, curled upon the bare mattress like an aborted fetus thrown away, her hands between her legs, until she fell asleep. Freddie ran down the five flights of stairs and stuffed the filthy sheet into the garbage can in the alley beneath the building, carved into its brownstone belly, and then he huffed and puffed back up the five flights of stairs, and when he crashed open the door to the apartment he found Mona still heavily asleep, snoring, while Douglas and Doreen still sat clutching each other, still befouled by vomit, among the glass fragments on the floor, two dazed idiots who had shared a cruel dream, and Freddie announced to the room, through the fetid air, in a strangely accented rhythm, I love you, I love you, I love you, until he was able to listen awhile to the silence, to the deadly quiet between snores, between inhalation and exhalation, and he finally said, briskly, once more the man of action, "This shit has got to stop. Tomorrow, my friends, we are going to score. We are going back to junk. I mean, amigos, we have got to stay cool. We have got to. We have got to stay cool . . . ."

THE LIGHT FANTASTIC

Doreen danced.

Tuesday, morning. Window, grime-streaked, shadeless, opening on the east. Sunlight, catching the dust. Two stories below, school-children, working men and women, moving into the daylight from row houses down sandbrown steps. Across the street a morning breeze stirs curtains, pink and purple silk, yellowed lace, tacked-up towels and sheets. Pigeons gurgle on the ledges and crannies over-head. Traffic makes noises.

Doreen is hit by consciousness, abrupt and welcome. Black curls of Douglas across her arm, his guttural breathing against her breast. Lie still, girl. How awake eyes are, glowing in thin cat face, exam-ining peeling plaster and rooftops opening to sky with impartial attention. Wooden table, arbitrary chairs, hotplate, washbasin, win-dow sun and sky, wall with covered bridge calendar and pages torn from magazines, the elephant-headed god with consort, the cruci-fied god as infant with mother, two young women in a field at dawn, solarized. Doreen sees her home in the early morning, fully conscious, with Douglas at her side.

Doreen shifted her weight slightly, away from Douglas, and slid silently from the bed. She set some water to boil on the hotplate, reached under the bed for the two mugs, fetched instant coffee, sugar, powdered milk and a yellow dress from the closet. She dressed, rinsed the mugs in the washbasin, combed her hair, ran out into the unheated hall to the john, and returned to make a face at the slowly heating water. Snap. The radio poured out sound, music, beat, and Doreen danced. Barefoot on grey linoleum, barefoot in dust and sunstream, barefoot above the world five stories over the slow-breathing street a girl named Doreen danced for the morning. Douglas rolled over towards the sound and movement, opened his green gaze upon her, and almost felt joy.

"What are you doing?"

"Dancing," exultantly, "I'm dancing."

"It's been a long time since you've danced, Doreen."

"It will be a long time before I stop, Douglas." But she stopped. She collapsed, laughing, onto the bed, onto him, her mouth nipping at his chest, her hair trailing over his belly. "I'm still dancing," murmurs and caresses, sudden warmth.

"My coffee, girl."

Over coffee, sobriety punctuated by giggles, the unmade bed holding unfulfilled promise, "Today, Douglas, we'll look for work."

"What's gotten into you?" He is almost feeling joy.

"We're clean. I'm alive. I want to dance. I woke up this morning and everything was here. I was seeing the daylight. We're clean. Dig it, baby, we're never going to shoot junk again. Never. This time is for real."

Her face was almost new, her eyes alight, her cheeks flushed. He looked upon her and a shadow moved across his heart.

"So we're going to get straight gigs, huh? I'll clerk in a supermarket and you'll do filing in an office where you'll water the philodendrons and fetch the coffee. We'll save a little money and you'll take a few courses at night, learn to type. You'll become a typist in the office pool and with your looks and brains in no time at all you'll be a secretary. An executive secretary. Meanwhile with my looks and brains and a night school course in industrial psychology or something I'll work my way up to store manager. My organizational talents being recognized, I soon will be vice president of the company. We'll buy a vine-covered cottage a white picket fence a station wagon a dynamite sports car and we will have children.

A boy and a girl, of course. I will take out a sound insurance policy and you will join the PTA and canvass for the heart fund. In the summer we will take vacations. The boy and girl will go to a brother and sister camp."

As he spoke she nodded and smiled, but the shadow grew larger and darker and she, watching his glittering eyes, grew bewildered and apprehensive. He rattled on, his lips twitching in a smile she feared.

"We will buy a nice cemetery plot and in our middle years we will visit it and gaze upon our square inches of green grass surrounded by the white tombstones of others who prudently bought cemetery plots and we will listen to the silence, straining to hear bird calls, but we will hear only each the other breathing, life rasping noisily in our nostrils. . . ."

"You're crazy. You talk like that because you're crazy."

"I talk like that because I'm crazy, Doreen mavourneen."

"Finish your coffee and get dressed. We'll buy a newspaper and look for work."

"I've finished my coffee, my lass, and I'm ready to go back to bed with you."

"Later for that. We are getting straight gigs, and we're getting out of this junkie hole. As soon as we have some money we're moving to a nice neighborhood. Get dressed."

He took her to bed and he got dressed and together they shared the want ads, sitting on the steps of a building much like their own. A few houses down a man was drinking wine from a bottle hidden in a brown paper bag. It was 9:30, still a Tuesday morning. The neighborhood stoops were beginning to fill with nodding junkies, with women and their babies, men and their out-of-work worries,

nodding junkies, wide-lapped grandmothers, ambulatory tuber-
cular cases, nodding junkies. Douglas and Doreen circled help
wanted ads with a new pencil, and took the downtown subway to
the agencies.

That evening Douglas had a job and Doreen hadn't, but she had a
bouquet of flowers that Douglas had brought home, along with an
alarm clock that he had lifted.

"You can't lift things any more. You're clean now. Only junkies
steal."

He wound the clock, grinning.

By Friday Doreen had a job too. The weeks began to pass. On
Friday nights they bought wine. On Saturday nights they went to the
movies. Doreen still sometimes danced in the mornings. At night
her face was strained and pale. Douglas watched her, waiting. They
fought at times. Douglas lifted filmy nightgowns for her, patterned
scarves, costume jewelry, perfume, cosmetics, gloves, a sweater.
She'd be cross but she'd be pleased. "Only junkies steal," laughing,
stroking his curly hair.

A month later, perhaps five weeks, Douglas came home with two
women's magazines, a six-pack of beer, a sack of pretzels, and
found Doreen overdosed, sprawled on the floor, the needle next to
her. He methodically pounded her face with his open palms, praying her name. He hauled her to her feet and marched her around the
narrow room, pinching the flesh of her underarm, smacking her lax-
muscled face. Her eyelids fluttered open and she sought his green
eyes, sought his forgiveness. He had forgiven her weeks ago. He
threw her into a chair. She stumbled to her feet and headed blindly
for the bed, to fall out, to dream again, but he forced her back into
the chair.

"Well, you're not dead."

"No, I'm not dead. I wasn't even going to nod out, baby. I was just going to get a little high. You wouldn't even see me nod. I didn't want you to know."

"It's been a long time. How much did you do?"

"Just a ten cent bag."

"Must have been dynamite."

"Mmmm." She was nodding. He moved her onto the bed and took off her shoes and stockings. "Thanks, baby. Everything's cool." He sat down next to her, examining her fine-boned face, the hollow of her throat, the swelling of small breasts beneath the yellow dress, the one she had so blithely donned and danced in those few weeks ago. He drank a can of beer, undressed and lay next to her. He examined the ceiling with eyes that burned with the dryness that years ago had replaced tears. That night he slept with the light on. In the harsh glow their faces grew gaunt in sleep, trapped beneath the light.

In the morning she tried to explain, telling him of the frustrations at work, the various cruelties that had been inflicted upon her during the day, the horror of the subway ride home, the blinding headache, the junkies lining the stoops on her walk from the station. He drank his coffee, glanced at the clock. Together they left for work.

Evening. Spring air and guitar music brightening the treeless street. Douglas and Doreen, crouching in a narrow room, avoid one another's eyes. The walls close in upon them. They see the pit. Sleep is alien, impossible, the streets are dangerous, thought is hell. Two people in a narrowing molecule of the universe, each afraid of knowing each other, trembling away from the contact of mind, lose themselves in a clash of bodies. Their sexmaking is violent, bitter and brief, bringing a dull despair, coaxing consciousness into leaden sleep.

The gadfly hum of the stolen alarm clock collided with strangled dreams. Among the other grey slugs of the world they crawled off to work, their eyes sandstung, their mouths slimy with the nickel aftertaste of coffee. Daffodils bloomed in the florist shops. There was nothing to look forward to in those days of cement and clock hands except the evenings.

Another evening Douglas threw two bags on the table. Doreen added her two bags. She shot up first. As she lay on the bed, leafing through a magazine, he eased the spike into a vein from which the track marks were beginning to fade. He didn't shoot, he just eased the needle in and out of the vein. She watched in disbelief.

"Shoot, for god's sake. Why don't you shoot?"

"Doreen, do you believe in god?"

"What?"

"Do you believe in god?"

"I don't know. What are you talking about?"

"God."

"God. No man, I don't believe in god. Are you crazy?"

"Must be. I believe in god, Doreen." He shot up.

The first day they missed going to work they went shoplifting together. It was like old times. He bought her flowers, daffodils, to match her yellow dress. The day they decided never to go back to those dumb straight gigs they picked up on a little cocaine to mix with the junk, for a real good head. Time disappeared.

Time disappeared. Doreen and Douglas disappeared.

In the warp of reality into which things and people sometimes stray appeared two angels sharing a halo in the shape of infinity. One angel believed in god, he said. One angel didn't believe in god, she said, spreading her legs to a man, to men, for money to buy more infinity for her halo. The other angel felt his eyes burn, a dry flame that saw everything, and then he nodded out and saw dreams he would never remember, never forget.

"Forgive you?" each almost touches the other. "There is nothing to forgive."

The radio is playing. "How many angels, Doreen, can dance on the head of a spike?"

FATBOY

Fatboy stood at the river's edge between seven and nineteen, not sure which river it was. It could be the Mississippi, and he could be seven years old, a fat boy in St. Louis, in Missouri, where his father sometimes found work in the shoe factory, when he felt like working. But it might be the Hudson, and he might be nineteen years old and no longer fat, but still Fatboy, and on Manhattan's West Side, where his father didn't work at all, but sat home all day playing solitaire and living on the welfare, sparing the city the expense of hospital maintenance by not trying to kill himself every payday. Either way he was only sure that he was Fatboy, the fat boy who wouldn't get lost. The river was as brown as anybody's river, and flowed from away past here to somewhere, which is what rivers are for. The water caught light and carried it elusive nowhere, which is what water is for. Deep down was mud, unseen. Elsewhere was where he was, whether he was man or boy. Here he was always fat. Man overboard. Buoy in the water. Lifeboy, man overbored. A gull screamed. Seagull, ocean, Hudson, New York, nineteen, man, no longer fat, Fatboy. I never think about killing myself, Fatboy decided. I'm not seven years old. The old man cheated and the solitaire hand came out. There were no more paydays, and the sunshine on the card table was seven years old.

Near St. Louis the Mississippi River and the Missouri River flow together, redbrown to the Gulf of Mexico. A little boy could see many things in the steady flow south. Mostly Fatboy saw blood, blood within an encasing vein moving life through the body returning to the heart; blood of many armies spilling, "rivers of blood"; menstrual blood half-glimpsed half-understood on a discarded sanitary napkin. Mother's blood, rust against billowy white; his mother's hair, redbrown against the white pillow, she smiles in her sleep. Fatboy's own blood secret and male within his inner rivers yielding to the world if his flesh yielded to enemy maleness, to danger and switchblades swords arrows and fists. His flesh would never yield, however; the secret rivers of his blood were sheltered deep beneath layers of fat, cushioned between the crux of him and the cudgel of them.

Fatboy turned from the river and looked toward the city. A cold wind blew from the water. He turned up the collar of his jacket. The rising needlepoints of buildings assaulting the sky held a message for his veins. His blood called back and the river carried the filth of the city to the sea.

Harry and Fatboy looked alike, Fatboy liked to think. They had both once been fat, fat boys, fat men, and they both retained the solidarity that Fatboy appreciated as masculine. Of course, Harry was twenty years the older, but that was what made the similarity so intriguing, the reciprocal whisper of the future, echo of the past. Then again, Harry was fair, Viking-colored, as if his eyes held sea and his hair held sun and his skin held frost. Fatboy was ruddy, a permanent shame tingeing his cheeks, his hair, his hands. But his eyes too were blue, and they both had once been fat and now were men, thickset and strong, and there was a curve to the cheekbone that hollowed the face and a hunger slanting across the brow, thinning the lips, emboldening the eye, that made them look alike. Fatboy was content with the resemblance. They could have been father and son, he dared to think. He headed for Harry's as if he were heading for home.

Harry's wife had once been very beautiful, but she had never known it. She had passed from the shelter of her family to the shelter of Harry, and from the shelter of Harry to the shelter of his shadow. She still appeared virginal, and in her old age her eyes would retain the purity of a child, a child starved and beaten and trusting. Now she was Harry's wife, and sometimes he knew her as that, and most times she was faintly there, a ghostwoman once beautiful, who tried to warm herself in the chill of his shadow. She never knew that she was she, nor did anyone else, not husband nor children nor Fatboy.

"Is Harry here?" he asked, standing in the doorway, looking beyond her to the empty room ahead.

"He's still sleeping. Come on in, Jimmy. You look like you could use a hot cup of coffee."

"Yeah, I do." He shut the door gently, so as not to wake Harry. "I've been down to the river."

"At this time of year?" She disappeared into the kitchen, a dim cavernous room on an airshaft, a room that only she used.

Fatboy, could he have, would have sat at Harry's bedside until he awakened, watching over the older man's sleep. Instead he moved into the empty room, where he straightened newspapers, smoothed the throw on the couch, picked up a child's toy or two, and emptied ashtrays into the wastebasket beneath Harry's desk. It was the desk that Fatboy loved about the room, the desk that was Harry's office. It covered the length of one wall, bearing a row of fat textbooks, a miniature aquarium, a terrarium, potted plants, and was strewn with papers, all highly important and not to be touched by anyone but Harry. Harry edited a scientific publication, wrote for other publications as well, some scholarly, some popular, and was fond of lecturing to family and friends on the mystery of life. A human skull leered in the far corner of his desk, encrusted with the wax of many a candle, burned not for illumination but for effect. A typewriter was squatting dead center, before which a massive oak chair was set.

On the wall a butterfly collection, illustrated charts representing the musculature, skeletal frame and gastrointestinal system of the human body, and a large Grosz print, were displayed. They were jumbled together, leaving a wide expanse of wall to which a small pen sketch was taped, slightly askew. It represented a dead man sprawled at the bottom of a flight of stairs, a needle protruding from the arm. It had been drawn by a friend of Harry's, an artist who had mailed it one Sunday morning, to return home, overdose, and die. The sketch arrived in the mail the day of the funeral. It was a self-portrait. Harry had shown it to Fatboy, lent him a dark sport jacket, and before leaving the house for the funeral they had both mournfully, ritualistically shared a short length of straw, snorting from a pile of white powder laid out on a glossy-covered book of Titian reproductions. That was six months ago. It was Fatboy's first taste of heroin, and his first funeral. He remembered the day as one of solemnity and pleasure, of acceptance, of real masculinity. He liked Harry's desk, liked the mystery of the books, the jumble of words that encompassed all human knowledge, all science, all perception of the world, Harry's world. Organic chemistry, biochemistry, celestial physics, gold-printed on fat bindings. Fatboy yawned. He wasn't sleepy, but he yawned. Harry's desk and Harry's wife making coffee for Fatboy and Harry still sleeping going on two in the afternoon and the river all combined to make him yawn, and then he yawned again and recognized that in a few hours he would be junk sick and he really wanted to get stoned as well. The coffee was brought in and Harry's wife scuttled back to her cave, where she could sit and read about the Etruscans while supper stewed on the range.

Harry awoke and his wife brought him coffee and the newspaper that she had bought and read that morning and that Fatboy had straightened out that afternoon. She told him Jim was in the living room. He told her to send him in. Beaming, Fatboy walked in. Harry, unshaven, naked in tangled sheets, didn't look up. "Hand me my pants," he mumbled through crumbling toast. Fatboy jumped for the pants. Harry pulled his wallet out from a pocket, counted two hundred and thirty dollars twice, handed Fatboy the thirty dollars and said, "Run over to Dinah's and get a half-load. And bring me back some orange soda." Fatboy shoved the money in his jacket pocket and left. As he closed the door he heard Harry yelling, "Shut off that damned light in the kitchen. It's two o'clock in the afternoon. You don't burn electric lights at two o'clock in the afternoon." Fatboy knew that Harry's wife would shut off the light without a word. After all, it was two o'clock in the afternoon. Fatboy would shut off the light without a word too. He respected Harry.

Scoring at Dinah's was clean. She wasn't bad-ass, like Luis two flights down, and she wasn't anxious and lonely like Tillie across the street, and she wasn't a beat artist like almost everyone else.

"This for Harry?" she asked.

"Me and Harry, yeah," Fatboy answered.

"Yeah, well, tell him it's dynamite this time, to take it easy on it. Hey, Fatboy, here's something for you. It's for you, understand?" She pressed a bag into his hand.

"Thanks, Dinah." He felt himself blushing.

"I don't do this all the time, dig, and I don't do it for everyone. I just got a good count, and good shit, and I can afford it. The rest of this stuff is going to go out cut, dig it, but Harry got it just the way it came in. You tell him that."

"Sure. Thanks a lot."

"You want to do that bag up now? It's for you. You can use my works." She was smiling, but she seemed tense. Fatboy didn't know what she wanted. He shook his head, not knowing what to do. "I don't want to carry while I'm high. I'll wait till I get home."

"Back to Harry, you mean."

"Yeah, back to Harry." Fatboy left. At Harry's door he realized he had forgotten the orange soda, and walked back two blocks to buy it. He paid for it out of his own money. He went home, back to Harry.

Fatboy handed the half load over, felt the extra bag in his pocket, pulled it out, and laid it on the table. "From Dinah," he said. Harry looked up at him. "What's the matter with her?"

"I don't know."

"Mmm. We'll split it, okay, Jimbo?"

"Okay."

Harry did up four and a half bags and Fatboy did up a bag and a half and they watched the end of a football game on television and Harry said it was time for Fatboy's chemistry lesson but after fifteen minutes of plodding through a college review book Harry's children came home, talkative and hungry, and Harry was too bored to continue, especially with the kids running around making noise and Harry said, "Come on, we have to move this shit," and Harry and Fatboy tapped the bags, replacing a little junk with a little milk sugar and taping the bags up again, putting the salvaged heroin in an envelope in a drawer for later and then they got ready to go out and Harry's wife said, "Dinner's almost ready," in *that* tone of voice and Harry said, "Keep it warm," and then Fatboy and Harry were moving, drifting through the streets finding Harry's people, and everything was good and warm and right and masculine.

Most of Harry's people were young, most of them had chippie habits, not yet junkies, most of them had money to spend, but not that much money, and Harry found them at home. He would pull out his half load and flash it and pull out his two hundred dollars and count it and add their three bills or five bills to his wad, and they would talk a little and move on again. When they got home the kids were in bed and dinner was warm and Harry's wife was talking on the telephone and Harry did up two more bags and laid another bag on Fatboy and then they nodded for an hour, close together, and then Fatboy straightened up again, emptying ashtrays, taking out the garbage, and Harry's wife thanked him. He wanted to ask if he could sleep on the couch again but he decided he would rather stay there tomorrow, and tonight would take care of itself. Harry was still nodding when Fatboy tiptoed out. It was Sunday night, and cold, and the streets were empty. He began looking for an empty garage, an unrented apartment, somewhere to sleep. He wound up on the stairs leading to the roof in a walk-up brownstone. It was cold on the stairs, but the streets were colder yet, and Monday night he would sleep on the couch.

By the summer Fatboy was sleeping on the couch every night. It was warm, of course, and not as bad to make one's bed on a stairway or rooftop as in winter, but the streets were crowded, often till one or two in the morning, people were on the move, too heat-restless to stay at home. It was nice to sleep in the parks or on the beaches, too, but there was a risk of being rolled by other junkies, pulled in by the police for vagrancy, or beaten up by city-crazy packs of kids. Fatboy slept on the couch every night.

In return, he made himself useful. He babysat, swept, ran errands, washed dishes, took the laundry to the laundromat, and continued to empty ashtrays, take out the garbage, pick up toys. In exchange for picking up Harry's consignment of junk and delivering bags to Harry's people he got four bags a day for his own habit. Harry made the contacts, Harry put up the money, Harry did ten bags a day, and Fatboy did the running. A friend of Harry's taught Fatboy to take off stores and apartments, and Fatboy did a couple of jobs with him before going out alone, turning the money over to Harry to buy more junk. By the middle of August Harry was doing fifteen bags and Fatboy was doing six, and they both were very thin, as if father and son had both been in the same concentration camp. There were no more lessons from the college review books.

Harry and Fatboy sat on the edge of Harry's bed, staring out the window. Harry switched off the air conditioner and opened the window. "I'd rather listen to the sound of the streets than that mechanical monster whirring away," Harry said. Fatboy laughed. They gazed from the heights of the fifteenth floor down at the huddled brownstones in the streets below, squat five-story walk-ups peppered with heads yearning from open windows.

"There must be five hundred junkies on that street," Harry said. Fatboy laughed again. "Five hundred junkies, Fatboy. On one street.

Think about it. And they're all worms. Blind ignorant worms. Listen to them." Fatboy listened. He heard traffic, radios, guitars, children, mothers calling. "I don't hear any junkies," he finally said.

"Of course not," Harry answered. "Junkies are very very quiet. What you hear are people who are going to be junkies. That stickball game. Those little kids on the steps. That young girl screaming at her boyfriend. All junkies. Some day. Junkies are very very quiet." He closed the window and turned on the air conditioner again. "You should get to know some young people your own age. Be good for you. Like those kids downstairs, playing stickball. You need friends your own age." Fatboy was confused. He was afraid Harry was tired of him. He looked pleadingly at Harry. It was Harry's turn to laugh. "And those kids your own age, Fatboy, need junk. It'll cool them out. They need junk, Fatboy, lots and lots of junk."

By the time that summer had ended and the school year began, Fatboy had lots of friends his own age. They looked up to him. He had the good connection, he had the junk, he and Harry had money to feed their big habits. One night Fatboy had a dream. He dreamed that Harry was tattooing him all over his body, tattooing HARRY on his chest, his arms, his buttocks, his rosy cheeks, and every prick of the needle was getting him higher and higher. He awoke in the night, almost screaming, to discover that the force of his dream had polluted the couch. He did up a bag, hands shaking, and at three in the morning walked to the river. The water was black, the color of the blood of a strangled dog. His hands were still shaking. He pulled out his switchblade, the one he had bought when he started taking off apartments, and carved Harry's name in the rotting wood. He was at the river's edge again, at the edge again, still not knowing who he was, not as young as he might have been, remembering the color of his mother's hair, his mother's blood, feeling fear under his high. A man was walking towards him, and for a moment he thought it was his father, coming to punish him for his thoughts, and then he realized it was just a night crawler, a pier walker, lonely for some cock in the night. The man began talking to him, and Fatboy didn't understand the words, didn't hear the sounds, but he saw the money and he nodded yes.

Between his legs the man was small, a worm, one more worm, his blond hair dry, dead against Fatboy's belly, bleached hair and cold hands gripping Fatboy's hips and warm mouth asking something of Fatboy's sex and Fatboy, lazy through the junk, pulled his mind away from the stranger and his strange demands and floated with the river, the blood of the earth, carrying the filth of the city to the sea, to his heart, and what he desired merged with the river, a mother-river, a father-river, a man-woman river, a Harry-river, a power-river, a death-river, and between Fatboy and desire stood the junk. It was no good. He couldn't get hard. The little man with the bleached hair and the dark pock-marked face looked disgusted. "What's the matter with you?" the worm asked, and this time Fatboy heard the sounds, understood every word, "You a fag or something? you're not even hard, faggot."

They were foolish words from a little man at three o'clock in the morning after a frightening dream on a deserted dock with a man-boy who had once been a fatboy and was still big, still masculine, and Fatboy's mindhands fastened of themselves on the fragile wind-pipe and crushed the words out of the worm, and Fatboy's mind-knife carved Harry's name on the deadman's belly and Fatboy fed the crumpled flesh to the river. Or he thought he did, running. . . .

Fatboy stayed with the river, walking upstream, until dawn. He walked into the morning of the city, vaulted a subway turnstile as the train pulled in, and rode back downtown, home, to the tattoo artist Harry. Humbly he entered the kitchen and found Harry's wife giggling as she made coffee. Harry was standing next to her, his hand under her skirt. He grinned at Fatboy, his hand lingering under his wife's skirt. "Up early, huh, Fatboy? Been tomcatting around?" Fatboy began to sob, and he found himself locked against a strong shoulder, embraced by a strong pair of arms, and a man's hand was pushing the hair out of his eyes, his mothercolored bloodbrown hair.

The fingers smelled of warmth and female like the blood on the sanitary napkin that haunted his years. Fatboy retched. "I'm choking!" he cried, "I'm choking!" and Harry rushed him to the window. "Fresh air," Harry said. "No, not like that!" Fatboy screamed, "Inside I'm choking! Inside me, Harry, inside me. Oh, cut me open, I'm choking!"

The two men, sharing the same hunger darkening the eyes, hollowing the cheeks, thinning the lips, held each other at the open window, two strong men, once fat, broad of chest, solid-thighed, and their flesh melted towards each other, two men, one man, hungering, one flesh, and Harry's wife saw in her kitchen writhing by the window opening on the airshaft a puddling of flesh, a manmonster, an enormity waving arms and legs, a oneness, a masculine force no longer Harry nor Fatboy, and she opened her mouth to scream but remained silent, imprisoned in her terror as the manmonster struggled at the window, pushing towards the open air, the sky, pulling back, oozing out the window, wrenching back, and then the manmonster was Harry and Fatboy fighting, one pulling the other out the window, and she screamed as Fatboy screamed, hurtling fifteen stories downward, while Harry rested his head against the wall, breathing hard. "Stop screaming," he rasped. She stopped screaming. He closed the window, not bothering to look down. "One more dead junkie. He must of fell from the roof. How the hell did he get in this building? The front door is always locked." He sipped his coffee, listening for an approaching siren, while she cowered away from his shadow, trapped in the terror of her awakening.

THREE STREET KOANS

If only I knew the answer to this one question I have asked you, master, then would I find enlightenment.

And what was your question? answered Shogen.

At this Douglas was not enlightened.

Mumon's comment: Shogen and Douglas exist at different moments of spacetime. How then did they converse? Could Douglas's question have been Shogen's enlightenment? Do any of us believe ourselves? What am I talking about?

Douglas experienced lightning Zen. Shogen, Mumon, Joshu, Kyogen, all you Zen masters, you're all full of shit. Jesus winked and twinkled at Douglas from the storefront church. For if I build again the things I destroyed I make myself a transgressor. For I through the law am dead to the law, that I might live with god. Ah, Saul, Paul, do you preach through those painted eyes that fine Jew logic? Damn it, I'm not a Jew. Eli, Eli, lama sabach thani, the marimba band screamed.

Hey Pablo.

Hey man.

In front of the gaudy god Jesus Christ the two men shook hands. Thirty pieces of silver bought a half load, and they burst apart, their humanfleshed fragments moving away from one another, negative-negative repulsion, toward their own karmas. Jesus smiled at the empty street. Nothing very significant about this. He smiled at everything. He was designed to smile, a laughing Buddha, slightly swish. The women liked him that way.

Douglas moved fast. His people were waiting. Oh, they knew how to wait. They had sat hunched in their clothing waiting in welfare offices, hospital clinics, legal aid anterooms, jails. Now they were waiting for the man. But Douglas, not a social worker or doctor or lawyer or cop, didn't say fuck them, let them wait. He moved toward his people, salvation in his pocket.

They waited bonelessly, draped upon the furniture, decadent Rome. There was no conversation, little talk. Freddie thumped his knife into the soft wood of the kitchen floor, too tired to fantasize killing. Mona paced from table to sink, almost washing the dishes. Cat-faced, Doreen nibbled at her nails. The others moved even less, jiggling a leg, chewing a lip. The radio was snapped on, twisted through its stations, snapped off. Karen, tangle-haired and jungle-naked, moved through the two rooms from one averted face to the next, sucking alternately at a baby bottle filled with Kool-Aid and the heel of a loaf of West Indian sourdough bread. She avoided Mona, her mother, as she was expected to when mother was "nervous".

Douglas slammed open the unlocked door, and the room closed in upon him, bees about a grinning flower. Activity sharpened the corners of the furniture, whittled the tense bones of faces. Some one locked the door. Beasts pawing a corpse, snouts dipping into bloody innards. Coin for junk, junk for coin. The gas jet ignited, the blue flame round and mystical crowded around, primitives drawing near fire. Douglas's people jostled one another, spoons extended cooking powder into syrup, sweeter than honey to the veins, to the hunger. In a corner of the living room Fatboy with his chippie habit snorted his stuff. Waiting to feel it, he watched the others in varying stages of getting off cooking, tying, hitting.

There was no reason to leave, so everyone stayed. Once more, decorative, they masked the angularity, the thinness of the rooms, with their bodies, flesh draperies. The pattern once more etched, ritual of salvation, mandala, DNA, crystal, cosmos, sociology, enacting their thing, grace note of the race. Freddie again thwacked his knife into the soft wood of the kitchen floor, no longer waiting. Mona lost her air of being almost about to wash the dishes. She tossed a pair of overalls at the kid. Get dressed, Karen. You'll catch cold running around like that. Obedient, bored with warm Kool-Aid, Karen wrestled with the overalls. Doreen watched her man from under shadowed lids. Don't do that, Douglas. Make your hit.

Grinning, sliding the needle into the blackened vein, easing it out, not shooting, Douglas gave his green eyes to the room, to the smudged faces. To join them, to be them, to blur out of spacetime, to enter the spectrum of now... power rested in the pressure of a fingertip, in the mockery of a grin, in the watching of the green of an eye. Power, non-power, awareness, non-awareness, in, out, Jesus or Christ. Shogen, have you answered my question?

The answer was before the asking, Shogen repeated. Why have you not heard my answering as you thought?

Mumon's comment: Shogen is jiving with Douglas. He knows but knows not, answers but does not give. This is not Zen, this is life. The wise man has not been born. Does this suffice?

I'm still taking notes, Doreen, Douglas winked and twinkled, ablaze in the muted room. I'm still finding god for you.

Why? crackled Freddie. Is he giving smack away?

Is that god? asked Douglas.

Hit, Douglas.

Is that god?

Yeah, that's god.

Heroin is god?

Yeah.

I thought god is love.

God is shit.

God is love or shit? Douglas wanted to know. His questions rolled through the room, disturbing the dust. What is god. Do you believe in god. Why. Why not. Define god. Can you weigh god, cut god, sell god, shoot god. What is ecstasy. Is ecstasy an up head or a down head. Why do you use junk.

Uneasily, they answered.

Just give me the right answer and I'll get off. I just want a few answers, that's all.

They answered. I think... I get high because . . . god is . . . if there was a god . . . if there wasn't god . . . ecstasy is. . . .

Fatboy made jokes. Douglas laughed to encourage him, to encourage the boy telling jokes against his fat self, his greasy soul. Jokes and answers and Douglas and his laughter. Douglas stiffened suddenly, plunged the needle deep, shot relief through his blood into his hammering pulse, until he was pressing emptiness. He held the needle in place, eying without irony the blood trickling into his palm creating the illusion of crucifixion. Okay people, no more god. You got all the answers. Doreen sidled toward him, cream-tongued, to massage his neck and tumble his hair, her lank body defending him from the overripe air. He allowed her to remove the needle from his vein.

Mommy, I'm hungry.

Mona hugged the little girl, pecked at her cheek. Later. I'll get you something later.

Now.

No, in a little while. Go look out the window.

I'm hungry.

Look in the refrigerator.

Nothing there.

Nothing? Mona sighed, rose, and went into the kitchen. Nothing there.

Goddamn it, who ate the bread?

Me, Mommy.

Well, Jesus, that's why there's nothing there.

I want more.

I'll go out later. You have to wait. Her voice grew shrill, edgy.

Doreen clapped her hands. C'mere, Karen. Come on, honey. Come sit on Doreen's lap.

Karen ignored her. I'm hungry I'm hungry I'm hungry the wail continued persistent and hopeless.

Drink your Kool-Aid.

I'm hungry. The chant became a sob, then modulated to a long drawn plaint, wordless and rising.

I can't stand this Mona groaned through clenched teeth. She's driving me crazy. The despairing cry continued, accompanied by a rhythmic knocking of head against chair, heavy on the fourth beat.

Christ almighty. Mona found the sucked heel of bread, gave it to the child. Karen pushed it away, still crying. God god god, why can't I have a little peace. Mona drew her wake-up bag from her hip pocket, slit the cellophane, and went back to the kitchen to tap some shit into a fire-blackened spoon.

The child watched Mona cooking the stuff down over the flame. Food, Mommy?

Medicine. Douglas, give me your works. The mother quickly, nervously, filled the works. Douglas, hold her across your lap, head down.

You're going to spank her?

No, I'm going to hit her. Muscle shot. Make her shut up.

Doreen opened her eyes. You can't.

Don't be dumb. I do it all the time. Otherwise she'll drive me nuts.

Douglas scooped the screaming child up, turned her over his knee, pulled down her overalls. Mona moved in quickly, hit the needle sharp against the tense buttock, just as Doreen screamed Don't!

Shut up Doreen, Mona muttered, you're as bad as the kid. There, that should do it. The child struggled away from the circle of faces, hiking up her pants, rubbing her backside, still crying. Then she stopped running, stopped rubbing, sobbed once and stopped crying. She stood in the center of the room, confused.

Go look out the window baby, Mona said softly. The child blinked, then trotted obediently into the kitchen, climbed on the table, looked out the window. Freddie tucked his knife into his boot, left the kitchen, and moved into the living room. The little girl slumped onto the kitchen table. She pillowed her head on her arm, sucked her thumb, and looked out the window until her eyes closed.

Freddie stretched out on the floor, digging at a sliver of wood with his thumbnail. That kid's stoned out of her mind, he said. Gives me the creeps to sit with a three year old junkie.

Universal nod, out of time. The darkness came. Some one turned on a lamp and the radio, chasing shadows with electric harshness. Motion rippled through the sudden room.

Douglas, you gonna score again?

Not till tomorrow.

Mmm. Then I'm gonna split. Got some things to do.

Yeah, me too.

The room emptied. Douglas and Doreen curled together on the sofa, nodding undreaming towards one another. Freddie rose from the floor groaning, rubbing at the angles of his joints, and fell next to them. Mona padded to a chair facing them and sat on the edge, hunching forward.

Douglas, listen. I gave the kid too much from my bag. I'm gonna be short in the morning. Lay a bag on me, huh? I'll get you the money tomorrow.

Sorry, baby, Douglas lied. I only got enough for me and Doreen.

Leave me a taste out of your bag? Between the two of you I can get a little taste. You won't even miss it.

Tell you what. Soon as I score in the morning I'll bring you a bag.

No good. I won't sleep tonight unless I know I got it for tomorrow.

You'll sleep. I'll be here in the morning. Don't sweat it.

Shit, I shouldn't a given her so much. I hate being short.

The baby nodded out? Freddie asked.

Yeah, she's probably out in the kitchen on the table. She likes to sleep on the table.

Man, don't give me that. If I don't dig the floor, she don't dig the table. Hey you two, off the couch. I wanna open it. We'll put the kid to bed.

No, it's cool, said Mona. She digs the table. Her bones are still green.

Shit. Off the couch.

Douglas and Doreen rose, arms around each other, and stood swaying while Freddie dragged out cushions, unfolded the sofabed.

You could put a sheet on the bed, Mona, Freddie grumbled.

It doesn't matter. She just wets them anyhow.

The room stagnated. A rot as if of centuries slithered over the sag-bottomed chairs, the mattress belching forth from the sofa, the beaded curtains dressing the archway leading into the light-less kitchen. It snaked insinuatingly about the four frozen people, touched them, made them suddenly aware. It was, in a sense, the last of such moments. Too quiet, laden with vague emotion, bereft of memories, the rot narrowed the room, forced them closer together.

I'll get the kid. Mona brushed through the beaded curtains, her hand lingering on them as she passed. Caressing space, she moved from then to now.

Lightglare upon porcelain, cruelly unmasking the kitchen. Dishes unyielding in the sink. Window black upon the outside. Karen, tangle-headed young, crumpled on the table. The three in the living room listening to a motherly croon, Karen honey wake up. Mothervoice seeping into icelocked brains, a dream in a dreary pinkwalled room. Karen. Karen? A sudden cry, too swiftly stopped, the razor's edge. Then the sound of blows, battering the ears. Karen! thwack! Karen! thwack! sharp dull sharp dull, the frail body limp against the voice, the hands, the blows.

Doreen cringed against Douglas, against shoulders broader than her own. What's she doing? Why does she have to beat her like that?

Freddie, angry against his high, moving through the air like a knife, steel inside his boot pressing against his ankle, ran into the kitchen and grabbed Mona's arm.

Are you crazy? Leave the kid alone.

Let go, Freddie. I gotta. She won't wake up.

Life threatened. Douglas and Doreen hurtled into the kitchen as Freddie lifted Karen in his arms. All four, jolted from high, gazed at the category of death. All there was to see was a lolling head, the glint of white through half-closed lids, a purpled face with protruding tongue, motionless chest, ragdoll finality.

Gruffly, you're hitting a corpse, laying the child back on the table.

No. Cat Mona sprang towards the table, towards the childdoll crazy-limbed and unhungry. No. The voice traveled through the country of grief, to a lone high peak. The no filled the kitchen,

69

caromed from the corners, returned to the listeners. The others had to act. As Freddie restrained the cat woman mother, Douglas straightened the dead child's body, covering her swollen face with a dish towel. Because she knew that Douglas had more, Doreen was able to tear apart her wake-up bag. She cooked it down, filled up her works, and stood trembling before the stove, before the fire. She hit Mona with more shit than she was used to, with Doreen's own good shit.

They led her into the living room, lay her on the mattress, where the smell of piss loosened sorrow within her. She tossed and moaned, her fingers raking her hair, like a woman in childbirth. Her cries subsided and she wept, her pain burrowing inward so that her womb ached. The shit was dynamite. She nodded out. In the kitchen the three junkies sat with the corpse, planning the funeral. Doreen felt sick and vomited in the garbage pail.

The funeral arrangements were simple. They would wait until twelve, one o'clock, when the streets were empty. Doreen was to stay with Mona, hit her with another bag if she woke up. Freddie and Douglas would wrap the child in a blanket, weigh it down with whatever they could find in the apartment, walk to the docks four blocks away and sink the jail sentence in the river. There would be no eulogy.

When the men left, Freddie with a blanket pack slung over his left shoulder, Doreen felt in Mona's pocket until she found the half-filled bag, which she snorted. She hid the works and the extra bag under one of the loose boards in the kitchen. In case the two men were stopped, at least the place was clean. Her high had a new edge to it. She sat down beside Mona to wait.

What do we do now, she asked them when they returned, empty-handed, empty-eyed. It was a bad question.

There's nothing for us to do, Douglas finally answered. We're splitting.

Just like that?

Just like that.

Doreen retrieved her stuff. They left. Doreen, Lot's wife, saw Freddie lie down next to Mona, his arm sheltering her from the morning, as the door closed behind them.

Come on, Doreen, we gotta catch Pablo before he disappears.

Douglas, I gotta talk to you.

Talk, girl? You wanna talk?

I gotta talk to you.

Talk is just talk, baby. We gonna get stoned. We gonna stay stoned.

You believe in god, Douglas?

What do you know about anything? About god, about talk, about dying, about heroin? Don't talk, girl.

In front of the storefront church three men were standing, doing nothing. Douglas and Doreen stood there too, doing nothing.

There's a picture of god, Doreen. You believe in him?

I don't know. How could I? He looks so kind.

Bullshit. He looks like a fucking faggot. A smiling sonofabitch faggot.

Radiant, Jesus smiled at the man and woman leaning together, smiled at the houses leaning together, at the garbage cans leaning together, at the city, at the alley cat, at the river. His hands always blessed, his eyes always suffered little children to come unto him.

Pablo showed. The five closed on him, the mandala swirled, and cognizant flesh like flak exploded into the many directions of the sunless early morning. Douglas clutched his half load in his fist, grisgris against the weight of being.

Let's walk down to the river, Doreen.

Listen, Doreen, the river is talking to us.

Shogen told Douglas that he must go into the world. After many years, Douglas returned to the monastery gates. Shogen lay on his deathbed. Douglas knelt at the side of his master and wept. Do not weep, Douglas. Tell me about the world. Douglas spoke.

> Needle dreams shadowed and bare of color flicker
> through my nights. They are cold dreams, scavenger
> dreams. The hawk screams through city skies. In my
> dreams I am chased by spikes enormous as icebergs.
> Paralyzed by fear I wait for the white death to fall.
> The stars revolve in heaven; I am halfway through
> nothingness. I beg for the needle; befuddled by pain
> I watch it recede into its own infinity. I scream for a
> priest. Running I stumble across his skirted body
> dead of an overdose in the rooftop confessional.
> His wounded vein swallows the needle. His body is
> chewing him up. I am at the edge of the roof, a spike
> slams into the back of my neck . . . the dreams go on.
>
> Needle dreams. It's getting so bad I am afraid to
> shoot up, afraid to get high, afraid to nod into that
> amorphous world where menace and despair perform
> their classical charades. I am also afraid to stop.
> To all my charms add self-awareness. I offer

VI. THREE STREET KOANS

the deprecating grin, the scribble of irony my tongue
etches in the air between us, between any you and
cowboy me. Insights, firm ripe insights, who will
buy? I offer variety, commentary, all that jive, I am
the hipster, the jivester, the great white hope, my
right eye squinted against the upward streaming
smoke, rattling my small change and telling it,

ladies n gentlemen boys n girls, oh like it is.
Picture me and a shrink, dig it doctor I
don't want the cure I don't want to get at the
nitty-gritty I don't want to know why I don't
want to stop shooting I have found my life you
dessicated fart you thimblewit you Zen master
you asshole eater I just want the needle dreams
to go away make them stop hey don't you have
a brain pill to kill the pain?

Douglas my boy the pontificator pontificates,
all you do is jes eat the brains of a very old very
hip junkie. You jes eat his brains and the dreams
will stop.

Jeez doc thanx a whole million but where
do I find a spoon?

They say junkies know when they're going
to die. They run around frantic trying to clean up,
trying to make some girl, trying to get a straight
gig. They make a lot of noise and a lot of hassle
and then they sink back, weary, and try to stay
stoned. They look at every bag of shit they use
and they think it could be pure stuff or pure
poison, either way it can kill me. They never
shoot alone. They OD once, twice, and someone
always brings them back. Then they're found

dead in a place they've never been, and no one
knows whether someone dumped them there
because they couldn't be brought back or
whether they went to the elephant dying grounds
to shoot up one last time. They do say junkies
know when they're going to die.

Man, I've seen them dying, I've seen them
dead. They all look surprised. That's why I don't
pay any attention to feelings or dreams. I got a
place to live, a good connection, a woman good
looking enough to hustle good money.

When he fell silent, Shogen said, I don't understand.

How then can you die? asked Douglas.

As I lived, responded Shogen. Douglas, you must return to the
world.

No. I want to die here, as you do.

I am not a buddha, Shogen said, and he laughed. You are a buddha,
golden-faced one. The world is waiting for you.

Shogen died as he lived. Many have studied his words, the words of
an enlightened one. Douglas was sent from the monastery into the
world. With his fists he beat upon the locked gate until the blood
came. He held his bloodied hands out for the dogs to lick.

Doreen, what does the river say?

Rivers don't speak to me, Douglas. They only speak to you.

Oh. Know what the river told me?

What?

The river says it all sucks.
Yeah, well, the river don't know anything I don't know. But we're here, aren't we?

Oh yeah, the laughing Buddha said, we're here, sure as hell.

Mumon's comment: Shogen presumed to teach Douglas about life and death. Douglas is a reincarnated buddha, an all-compassionate one. He taught Shogen how to live in the world and die in the world. Why then did an enlightened man like Shogen choose the cloistered life to die in? This is not lightning Zen. Is Jesus a faggot? Is Saul become Paul a junkie? When Douglas said he wasn't a Jew, was he being a Jew? For if I build again the things which I destroyed I make myself a transgressor. For I through the law am dead to the law, that I might live unto god. What is law? What does Doreen mean by god? Is the story of Karen all the news that's fit to print? Ask the questions and think about law. Think of Douglas the golden-faced Buddha and stumble. I am afraid of this man.

DISCIPLE

Fatboy was sitting on the top step of a brownstone, blocking the doorway. He was sitting before the one tree of the block, a virginal maple that swayed shyly in the first warm breeze of spring. Fatboy watched the shivering of budding leaves and knew the tree would die, as the tree planted the spring before had died. Though the little dark man who had planted it would water it, would pack plant food at its roots, would surround it with chicken wire to ward off leg-lifting dogs and knife-slashing children, the little maple would die. Next spring the little dark man, grimly longing for a past home that was green but hungry, would cherish another sapling until it too drooped and faded. The heavy August, with its heat and gasoline fumes, would bring the stew to a boil, and one of the first deaths on a street of over two thousand souls, a street of two thousand bounded by two wide avenues, would be that of the little maple. Fatboy thought about death, about people dying. People did die. People would die. Old Mrs. Cohen, or Klein, or Kike, whatever her name was, would probably die. With all her locks and bolts and charms against the terrors, she would probably get her eggshell of a skull very bashed in one night. Fatboy considered doing it himself. They said she had a fortune hidden in her first floor front. But they always said that about the Jews. But she'd die. And Virgin Mary, a junkie whore grown suddenly older and uglier than her habit, would probably die. There were many possible deaths for her to die, but they all centered on her whoring and her habit. If Fatboy had his chance, if his dreams came true, a lot more would die. Throats throttled, eyes popping, knees going slack, was a good dream. It was said that Douglas had once choked a man to death, and he was only sixteen at the time. Time was slipping by; Fatboy was already seventeen and had never killed anything bigger than a kitten. From the mastery of hands crushing a windpipe he moved to the panther power, the pounce, the silence, the ripping, the blood. Smaller, meaner, the image of someone being held under water, the bubbles breaking at the surface, until the champagne of death went flat. Idly on, until the question of suicide intruded itself, Fatboy mused. His own death seemed an absurdity, a grossness in a delicate weave.

That he could die was possible, that he would die unthinkable. The tree shuddered before his eyes, the wind troubled his hair, and he stopped thinking. Once more, empty of inner image, he was only seeing a tree, a street.

A crackle of movement threatened Fatboy at the periphery of his vision. Turning suddenly to meet the suddenness that loomed larger than the quick darting of children playing, Fatboy saw Douglas moving rapidly down the block. No other adult moved that jauntily, with such purpose. If others were in a hurry, they scurried, ferret-like; if they had purpose, it was either furtive or futile. Douglas was going somewhere. The vagueness of somewhere had a terrible immediacy. Fatboy ran down the steps to meet him and started to walk with him.

"You in a hurry, Douglas?"

"No."

"Slow down, man. I'll walk with you." Douglas slowed his pace, smiled at Fatboy. Fatboy, encouraged, was able to nonchalantly ask him where he was going.

"Where you going?"

"Down to the river. Wanna come?"

"Yeah. Yeah, sure. I go there a lot too. Yeah, I'm down there a lot." There was a lot more to be said, questions that smoked with the asking, timid confidences waiting to be revealed, but Douglas commanded silence with his eyes and his smile, and Fatboy translated his own whimpering desire to please into respect. Silently then they walked to the river, to the rotting grey wood of the pier, to the waters brown with sewage. Fatboy felt unsurely that something was to be shared, but what it was was as unthinkable as the matter of his own death. The silence between them became uncomfortable. This, then, was a time to talk.

"Did you really kill a guy when you was sixteen? They say you choked a guy to death." There was no time to regret the question, to hear again the adolescent blurting, the uncontrolled tenor skittering too high out of its range. Douglas's answer was rapid, as was his walk, and as purposeful, and led to the same end. He spat into the river, and something happened to his eyes. They were at once surprised and weary, betraying too much as they warily clouded over. "Sit down," Douglas said.

The choice of place was unfortunate. Something stank, something foul had washed up against the pier, or had lodged in a niche between wood and water. Trapped by the odor of death, neither Douglas nor Fatboy could move, and there they sat.

"The trouble is, I really don't know, man. I mean, I told everybody I did, and I thought I did then, but afterwards everything got very confused. Then I started to dream things, and then I thought maybe I was remembering wrong, and then I thought I really was remembering wrong, and then I stopped trying to remember anything. So I don't really remember, and I really don't know. Did I kill a man? I don't remember. I don't even remember what I had for breakfast this morning."

Fatboy wavered between disappointment and a glimpse of something seen. Curiosity dominated. "You probably didn't even have breakfast."

"Probably not. I never eat breakfast."

"What did you remember when you first did it? When you thought you did it, what did you think you did?"

"I thought I jumped on this cat that was asking me too many questions and choked him to death. Then I ran away."

"Well, don't strangle me, man." Fatboy laughed. "You can just tell me not to ask any more questions."

"I'm not out to kill anyone. Jesus Christ. I don't even know if I ever did."

"What did it feel like?"

"You sound like you wanna kill someone yourself. You should, man. You'll never find out nothing by asking questions. It felt like I was in an awful hurry. You know. Like I had to get someplace in a hurry, and this was the way."

"Did it feel like sex? They say it feels like sex."

"Do you know what sex feels like?"

"Jesus, Douglas, what kind of question is that? Of course I know what it feels like. What do you think I am?"

"Do you think killing a man could feel like sex?"

"Yeah, in a way. Yeah, in a way it could. That's the way I imagine it."

Douglas tapped Fatboy lightly with his clenched fist. Fatboy tapped Douglas back, slightly harder. A truck had pulled up near them, and two thick men, one half a head taller than the other, began to unload cases from the back of the van. Douglas slung an arm over Fatboy's shoulders, and by bearing down heavy on Fatboy's neck, forced his head to his knees. Fatboy rolled from under him, and jumped upon him. They scuffled for a moment, and then Douglas grabbed Fatboy from behind, held him captive. The wind that had been blowing in from the water died down. The irregularity of their breathing was punctured by the dull thud of the cases as they were hurled from the truck to the ground. In the still air, in the rising warmth of their bodies, they could feel a promise of the stagnant summer to come.

"You never think about killing a woman, Fatboy?"

"Yeah, I think about killing a woman. Anybody. Let go."

"Is there more sex to killing a woman?"

"Get off me, man."

"Is there?"

"No. No, man. It's too easy, too quick, killing a woman. Sex needs time. Hey, get off me." Douglas let him go. The stench was unbearable. They began to walk upriver. The last crate bounced to the ground, hit a rock, and from the hole torn in its side little black handballs began to spill out, bouncing with no particular grace or pattern away from the truck, the two men, the liberating rock.

"Don't worry too much about killing. Sometimes it seems like you have to. Sometimes. Don't be in any hurry."

"I don't worry about it, Douglas. I just wonder when. I know it's coming, I know it has to come. I just wonder when." Fatboy looked very young to Douglas, very young and very clean. Fatboy's face, with its high color and buttery cheeks, innocent of beard, seemed androgynous. Douglas placed the flat of his palm against Fatboy's high set zygomatic arch, felt the hardness of bone through the yielding layer of flesh, rocked his hand gently, moving Fatboy's head to his own rhythm. Fatboy sent him a sudden sly glance, coquettish and wary, that Douglas realized, with a pang that approximated jealousy, was a practiced glance. Pederastic images teased Douglas; he felt as if the corners of his mind were ragged, revealing hints of mind beneath. Still in physical contact with Fatboy, he balled his hand into a fist, pressing his knuckles into Fatboy's temple. Fatboy flinched; Douglas turned away, kicked at a rock, feigned a blow at the empty air. Disturbingly, he saw spots before his eyes. Douglas hated seeing spots before his eyes.

He knew they were always there to see; once noticed, they were hard to unsee.

"Let's move, man." Douglas strode ahead, listening to the crunch his boots made in the gravel, to the thud they made on asphalt as he reached the pavement. Fatboy stared after him, thinking he was understanding something, feeling shrewd. In actuality he hadn't understood anything, he had only realized that there was something to be understood. He saw Douglas, slim and hardbodied receding with distance put between them, saw the slightness of his buttocks encased in well-worn jeans, saw the defensive hunch of his shoulders under the bulk of the leather jacket, and confused with the image of Douglas he saw Harry, thick-bodied in a sport jacket that well cut on the rack bagged and crumpled once worn.

Fatboy grinned. "Oh Douglas, man, you're so tough, you think you're so bad, but Harry's living up where the money is, with a better connection than you ever dreamed of, living high above the streets where all the money lives." He never would have dared say anything as brash, as uncool, aloud, but he grinned. Gauging the distance between them and feeling a prickle of alarm, he broke into a run and pulled up at Douglas's side, trying hard to conceal his labored breathing.

"Where you running to, baby?" Fatboy asked.

"I ain't the one that's been running," Douglas answered.

"Well, where you going?"

Fatboy left himself open. Douglas, compelled by trained necessity, looked Fatboy in the eye, let his gaze slide through Fatboy, cool and cutting. His stare worked like a scalpel; Fatboy, invaded, blushed. Douglas held his gaze. "Thought I'd sit down somewhere, have something to drink."

Fatboy scanned the street nervously. "You going in there?" He pointed to a bar across the street. It was a notorious pier bar, a rendezvous for men who needed men. Outside the doors, all night long and at lunch hour, studiously tough prostitutes with handkerchiefs padding their crotches posed for buyers. Downtown office workers and businessmen, with mid-day hungers, would grab a hamburger at a luncheonette and a mouthful of cock in the rented rooms above the bar. Fatboy felt he had made a clever and dangerous move. His blush had faded, he now was somewhat pale.

"I don't drink, man. Not that shit. All I want is a cup of coffee. Come on, Fatboy, I'll treat you to a lousier cup of coffee than you ever dreamed of." Again, he abruptly walked off. Fatboy was with him this time, his shoulders as hunched, his walk as slightly bowed. All the way to the diner everything was all right. They both were silent, feeling each within himself his own secret smile, his own sharing of time and hint of void.

In the future, another layer of the simultaneity interpreted as time, an historian was writing: In the twentieth century C.E. shortly before the Crisis of Perception, a perceptual movement swept the western consciousness, known in its own period as Pop, although later termed the Self-Consciousness Arrest. Its focus was on the mundane revealed, not with the aesthetic archness that characterized most realistic visions, but with a deliberate stripping away of any romantic notions, leaving only the acuteness of impression of artifact as artifact, person as artifact. In Pop, man saw himself as man-invented, along with the familiar artifacts of his culture. In the non-aesthetic fields, the same insight was manifesting itself. Anthropology was infected with the vision of Pop: human nature was defined as arising from the pressures of developing culture, human nature was seen as being delineated by the forms that man himself had created. Man therefore to the anthropologist was man-made, as to the artist, just as Being, for which the ancient word is God, was defined by advanced theologians of the declining Christian Era as also being man-made. In Pop the beginning of the

Crisis begins: theologians claimed that God was dead, anthropologists that man was culture-produced, artists that man was a machine. Thus the end was put before the beginning, humanity perceived itself as dead. At a point when the human race was first enabled to completely destroy itself with the use of nuclear energy channeled into Weapons (for a discussion of Weapons see Chapter Two, Aggression: Testosterone Unmodified), the Ubermenschgeist manifested itself particularly strongly in a racial spasm of the arts and other related fields. The human race gave up the ghost in order to avoid discontinuation. The Crisis of Perception was conceived; in the cradle of the womb of man's consciousness of death was God reborn, so to speak, springing full-blown from mankind's forehead. Wisdom was engendered from the skull, Love from the thigh, Compassion from the navel. So to speak. And we today (see endnote: Women). . . .

Et cetera. At a point that the human race was enabled to destroy itself with the use of nuclear energy, at a point prior to the Crisis of Perception, simultaneously with but not adjacent to the point at which a sincere historian was muddling hopelessly his metaphors, Douglas and Fatboy entered a small diner and in fluorescent glare became a part of a pulsating Pop tableau. They sat at a booth in the furthest recesses of the diner; the astringent odor from the men's room, a compound of urine and disinfectant, masked the smell of oil-fried eggs and potatoes that contributed to the Formica ambience of the place. Before them they saw a squeeze-tube of ketchup and one of mustard, a glass saltshaker dull with fingerprints, a metal napkin dispenser, empty, and a black plastic ashtray, full.

Douglas placed a crumpled pack of cigarettes on the table. Fatboy reached over and took a cigarette. He tapped it nervously on the table, pretending to tamp down the tobacco, as he had seen it done in the movies. The cigarette did not need tamping. He twiddled with the cigarette as Douglas rose. Douglas, relenting, threw a book of matches on the table just before he crossed to the counter. The counterman did not look up as he continued to wipe wet and dirty cups with a dishcloth. Fatboy struck the match against the matchbook five times before it took fire. Douglas ordered two coffees. "Make mine a Coke," Fatboy called. "Make that a coffee and a Coke," Douglas ordered. He leaned against the counter, his back to Fatboy. Fatboy straightened the cigarette pack, placing it parallel to the ketchup and mustard tubes. His color returned to his cheeks. He leaned into his seat, letting the smoke stream from his lips to his nostrils, to be re-inhaled. He noticed that he was tired. He didn't notice how good he felt. Douglas brought the coffee and Coke back to the table.

"Crummy place," Fatboy said. "Gives you salt but not pepper."

"Someone probably stole the pepper. This is a nice place."

Fatboy snickered. "Who would steal a thing of pepper?"
"Lots of people. Why shouldn't someone steal pepper?" Douglas too noticed he was weary. He also noticed that he was feeling good. He liked the river. He remembered the sound of handballs, black handballs, bouncing nowhere, and smiled.

"Sure, I guess someone might steal pepper. I can't imagine why, though. I wouldn't steal a thing of pepper."

"That's because you never needed pepper, baby. If you needed pepper you would steal it." Douglas took a tentative sip of his coffee, braced against its heat. It was lukewarm. "Lousy coffee."

"The Coke tastes like a cat pissed in it."

"What kind of cat?"

"A one-eyed grey and black striped Tom, working off a pussy hard-on."

"Yeah. That's the same cat that pissed in the coffee."

The counterman looked at them knowingly. Giggling. A pair of dope addicts, high on dope. Giggling like lunatics. He guessed he had them pegged. Fatboy jerked his head at the counter. "Dig the counterman, Douglas. He's staring at us like he thinks we're lunatics."

"Let him stare. He's got no one to look at but that old one-eyed Tom, and that cat's too mean to look back."

Fatboy felt depressed. The counterman kept looking at him. "Let's split, man. I can't drink this shit."

"No. I like it here. It's a nice place." Douglas admired the ketchup and mustard tubes, the three filtered cigarette butts and six unfiltered butts in the ashtray, the grey lettering spelling MEN on the greygreen door of the men's room. Other customers walked in, the counterman turned to them, ready to wink, to indicate with a nod of his head the two cokeheads sitting in the back, giggling. Fatboy relaxed again, feeling the weight of attention slink away from him, and drag itself with ponderous regret to the new customers. The depression lingered, a sour aftertaste.

"You know Freddie?"

Fatboy looked at Douglas with quickened interest. He knew who Freddie was. "Yeah, man, I know Freddie."

"You should talk to him. He's killed a lot of men."

"How you know? Does he talk about it a lot?"

Douglas yawned. "No, he never talks about it. But I can tell. I can tell from his hands. He's killed his share. But he thinks he killed more than his share. He hardly kills any more."

Fatboy whistled, low and silky. "That's a man for you. A real man."

Douglas drained the cold dregs of his coffee. "You think so, huh? You think that's what makes a real man?"

"That's macho, baby. To have killed so much you're tired of it. That's a man who's lived."

"No, man. That's where you are dead wrong. People always think that they can tell what a man is like by the way he handles other men." Douglas was suddenly serious. He came alive behind the green veil of his eyes, glowed forth vitality to reflect from the Formica, from polished steel and chrome. Fatboy was magnetized, held fast by the jasper of Douglas's eyes. He grew half tumescent but was contained by the heavy seaming and thick zipper of his jeans.

"No, man," Douglas continued. "Real macho is to be found in the way a man is with a woman. If a man really knows women, feels with them, if a man can second guess a woman, that's machismo."

Douglas was silent, the ideal of macho a marble rolling weightlessly along a level of his mind. He saw it so clearly. If a man is really in possession of his manhood, he is then a man most sensitive to women. It was a thought that didn't keep its place, a marble rolling along a level that kept tilting. Douglas grew dizzy with the tilt. The angle kept fluctuating, liquidating categories, dissolving edges that defined wholeness. He held precariously to his vision.

"See, man, most cats spend all their time trying to psych each other out. They're like animals forced together in too small a cage. Every move is survival. They don't realize that all they have to do to make room is to think it. The room is there in their own minds. But they keep circling each other, always ready for the kill. They never think beyond that. Well, beyond that is women, women and their woman-ways. And that is what is so far from men, something to be learned, to be truly conquered. I mean, if you know yourself you know other men, you know where they're at. There's nothing more to do. Keeping an eye out on other cats is like sleeping with one eye open. You're seeing something all the time, but asleep just the same. No, the thing to do is to dig women. That's what being a real man is all about."

Fatboy knew that Douglas was saying something that sounded important, but he still didn't know what it was. He decided not to think any further. He was disquieted by his own sexual arousal. "What you're talking about, man, is pussy."

Douglas let his eyes veil. He smiled, a crooked smile. His teeth were good. "Yeah, man. Pussy. But it's not as simple as that. Pussy is just an empty hole. It's nothing. But it's a hole in the center of the world, a peek into nothing. And that, baby, is something."

"Yeah, man, it's something all right."

Douglas regarded Fatboy thoughtfully. "Fatboy, you really need to get laid." Douglas stood up, walked to the door. Fatboy, excited and uncertain, pushed his Coke away from the edge of the table, rose, and followed him out the door. This time, he knew, they were really going somewhere. The river, the diner, the talk, were just a prelude. He had been right to run after Douglas in the street. Douglas was really going somewhere.

As Fatboy and Douglas climbed the stairs that led to Douglas's apartment, Douglas looked back at Fatboy, saying, "It's a nice place. They keep it clean here. No kids. They don't rent to kids."

Fatboy leaned against the wall, panting. The hallway wasn't all that clean. "Yeah. What floor you live on?"

"Fifth. Whatsamatter, you tired?"

"Why don't you live on the roof while you're at it?"

"Penthouse special. They only rent to pigeons."

The door was unlocked. Doreen was curled up in bed, hulking near the corner of the walls. She exploded when they walked in. "What took you so long?" She ran her tongue over her parched lips.

"It's a long story," Douglas shrugged. "Here's your stuff." He tossed a couple of bags onto the bed. She snatched them up, reached under the bed, and drew out her works. As she stood over the hot-plate waiting for the stuff to cook down she said, "You're not high."

"No. I decided to wait."

Fatboy said sententiously, "Never wait." It was a catch phrase, repeated by rote. He had not yet learned the urgency of its truth.

Douglas put another bag on the table by the window. "This is for you, baby. You got your own works?"

Fatboy, shamed, mumbled, "I don't shoot up."

"That's all right," Douglas reassured him.

"I just don't shoot up, that's all."

Doreen made her hit. She stared at Fatboy thoughtfully, again licking her lips. "You never shot up with Harry?"

Fatboy felt trapped. "Harry who?"

Doreen laughed. "Harry who?" she mocked. "Oh man, I seen you go in and out of that fancy building on the avenue at least a hundred times. Harry who. Your big dealer friend, that's who."

"He ain't no big dealer."

"All right, he ain't no big dealer. He's a medium sized dealer. With purple shades. Hey, how'd you ever meet him?" Doreen sank back

89

in the bed again, heavy with languor. She watched the color come and go in Fatboy's face, saw him glance nervously at the bag on the table. She found him funny, and decided he was okay.

"I used to deliver groceries to him. That's when I was into working square gigs. I was stupid then."

"Not so stupid," Douglas interjected in a lazy drawl. "You got to meet him. Man, I can't get to meet him."

"Yeah, maybe I wasn't so stupid. Hey, man, you don't have to meet him, you know, to do business with him. I'll do it for you."

"Good enough," Douglas said. "Want to shoot up now?"

Fatboy felt the trap loosen, then tighten again. He felt cold, felt the cool of beads of sweat breaking on his forehead. Doreen moved restlessly on the bed. "Come on, honey, shoot it. You can't stay a virgin forever. You just playing around the edges. If you do something, do it right. I'll do it for you, that okay? I'll shoot you up this time."

She didn't wait for his response. Without looking at him she slid off the bed, took his bag from the table, and began to tap its contents into a spoon. Fatboy looked away, caught Douglas staring at him. "I'll shoot up with you," Douglas said. He crowded next to Doreen, grabbing her ass as he did so. She arched away, complaining, "Hey, watch that, man, I almost spilled it."

Fatboy shivered, feeling very young and somehow naked. "Roll up your sleeve," Doreen ordered. Her breasts brushed against his shoulder. He rolled up his sleeve. "This ain't no doctor's office where you look away and get it over with," she said, tying a scarf around his upper arm. "You watch, man, because you got to learn to do it yourself. I ain't always gonna be around to do it, you know. A man gotta be able to take care of himself, you dig?" As she found the vein and pressed the needle, Douglas made his own hit, standing at Fatboy's other shoulder. Fatboy felt giddy, felt surrounded, felt he was going to swoon. "It's heavy," he mumbled.

"Yeah, well, it ain't like snorting. You get more for your money, you dig?"

All three crowded onto the unmade bed. Fatboy felt heavy and light at the same time, a constant oscillation of gravity that was as smooth as it was rapid. The velocity of spin slowed, then separated into levels. Light, heavy, speed, stasis, and then an even keel of pleasure with Doreen at his left, eyes closed, lips parted, and Douglas at his right, eyes half open and steady, lips pursed as in a kiss. Fatboy yielded, sank back against the wall, drifted. He was too smashed to be. Later, he returned to a somewhere that Douglas had led him to from a somewhere he had shared while alone to find Doreen's head against his shoulder, her hand light on his thigh, with Douglas sitting on a kitchen chair at the table, looking out the window. Fatboy wet his lips. Douglas, his back to Fatboy, tipped back in his chair and said, "How you doing, man?"

"I'm cool." Fatboy wanted to move, to join Douglas at the window, to hover close behind him and look out, look down, see outside. Doreen was an embarrassment to him, tendrils of her hair tickling his neck, her unconscious weight upon him bringing a tender responsibility that irked him, forced his desire to move. He tried to move her head onto the bunched up blanket where she could nod in comfort, but at the touch of his hands on her face she opened her eyes, smiled, and rolled over, her head now in his lap. Douglas tipped back in his chair again. "I'm cool too, man."

Fatboy shifted slightly on the bed. "That's pretty cool, Douglas."

"You still thinking about killing, Fatboy?"

"What? No, man. No, I'm not thinking about killing."

"What are you thinking about, Fatboy?"

"I'm not really thinking, Douglas."

Doreen opened her eyes. "I'm thinking," she said. "I'm thinking but I can't explain what I'm thinking about. It's like two ideas running together, but not exactly together. Like I'm thinking about what we're doing and saying now, and this room, and us in it. I can feel without looking the window and Douglas with his back turned away from us and the whole weight of the room, and I'm also thinking about inside me, inside my body and inside my head where it's all different from this room. But the two ideas aren't exactly together, you know? They get mixed up and then they get separate and then they get mixed up again. I can't explain it. I can't explain what I'm thinking about."

"Yeah, I know what you mean," Fatboy said. "I know what you mean. It's like two separate lives, inside and outside. You know you're here, but other things are happening and it's not here. It's inside and different. The time is different. But I can't explain it right either."

Douglas could see the sky above and the rooftops opposite, a grey sky soft and dirty, slashed by television antennae but unable to bleed, a wounded sky. "I see the sky," Douglas said. "I see the sky and the rooftops and laundry drying, hanging limp because there is no wind. I see smoke pouring from a chimney, smoke a darker grey than the sky. Behind me Doreen is lying with her head in Fatboy's lap. I can feel the two of you behind me, I can feel Fatboy's muscles cramped and uncomfortable from straining against enjoying Doreen's weight upon him. I can feel Doreen dissolving, disappearing from the room into her own dream. Doreen does that, Fatboy. She dissolves away when she yields herself. When you screw her she's not there at all, she's too busy getting away from the touch of your body into her dream. Her dream is that she's being touched by nothing, by the wind, by a warm sun that closes in on her and burns her to ashes. Her ashes are blown away by the wind, and then she says I love you. You believe me, Fatboy? You believe I know this room, know Doreen, know you? You believe me?"

"I don't know what you mean."

"Screw her, Fatboy. I told you you need to get laid. Screw her. She likes you."

Fatboy wished his heart would stop beating. He wished to live without being, without the steady pumping of blood through his body, through the corridors of arteries and veins, a labyrinth within his flesh. His body was never quite silent enough. The jostlings of red and white blood cells against one another were like the whisper of thunder. He hated this sense of danger, this danger without the clear excitement of physical menace. He resented being used. "You shouldn't talk about your girl like that. You shouldn't joke like that, man. It's not right."

"I'm not joking. Screw her. Christ, Fatboy, she's a hooker. She'll screw for love or money. Try her out, baby. Come on. The first one's free, kid. It's for love. After that you pay like everyone else."

Doreen, more silent than the rustle of Fatboy's blood, the sloshing of his digestive juices, the sliding open of valves within his body, began to touch him, to kiss him, her fingers as slender and tentative as the pattings of a child. The sexuality that had haunted him all day, that had pulsed in the flow of the river, in the bouncing of little black handballs, in the carbon dioxide escaping from a glass of Coca Cola, the gnawing desire that colored the sun a flaming red, deserted him. He felt cold, a child, cold against the chill caress of another child. "I don't know what's going on, Douglas, but I don't like it. What do you two want?"

"I don't want a thing, Fatboy. I want nothing. Nada. Doreen, she wants you." Doreen sat astride Fatboy, her hands cupping his face, her tongue snaking over his eyelids. He felt sexless, lonely. Douglas lit a cigarette, blew a smoke ring, blew smoke rings within smoke rings. Outside, the chimney stopped pouring forth smoke. Cinders flew wild in the air, rained upon the laundry limp upon the line. Doreen's kisses were quick and pale, her hands fluttered like moths against the shell of Fatboy's clothing, her fingers penetrated beneath his shirt, flicked his nipples, tugged at the hairs of his chest. "Douglas man, I can't do it with you here in the room. I mean, you want me to screw her, you gonna let me screw her, you gotta leave us alone. I can't do it with you here."

"What's the matter with you, Fatboy? I ain't even watching. I'm just sitting here in my chair, looking out the window. I don't care what you two do."

"I just can't do it with you in the room. It's making me real nervous."

"Okay, baby. You really need to get laid, I'm telling you, I know when someone needs to get laid. I'll go sit out in the hall." Douglas stubbed is cigarette out on the table top, then rose, crossed to the bed, kissed Doreen on the nape of her neck, and walked out, leaving the door slightly ajar.

Fatboy sprawled across the bed, passive beneath Doreen's imitation of passion. Fatboy regretted having insisted on Douglas leaving. He felt frightened of Douglas's absence, of the ghost of his presence still left in the room. Doreen was a vampire upon him, her sucking kisses draining him of manhood. he was unable to achieve erection, felt his body to be as it once was when he was very young, gross and blubbery, an insulation against the assault of the world upon his sense of self. His body was soft, womanish, his breasts fatty, the muscles undeveloped, his penis so small curled upon his testicles that it might have been an alien fragment of life, a small white grub that somehow had crawled between his legs. He was growing bloated, a huge white egg, while his penis shriveled, absorbed back into himself. He was grotesque, enormous, he was his own mother, he was an egg, he was his mother, he was melting, he was a river flowing pregnant with time, and as his eyelids closed upon his eyes he saw a strange light, blood-scented light seen through an eggshell. Doreen, as she felt his penis hardening smiled in triumph; she too dissolved, took fire, was consumed by a sun that burst within her, and in their clumsy coupling they both were set adrift. The mattress was overly soft, thin and lumpy, the bedsprings whined with Doreen's whines, and Fatboy, weak-thighed, was pinned beneath her, unable to answer her spastic writhings; he remained motionless, an egg sucked up by a self-destroying star. His seed was expelled in a series of low-pressure spurts. They fell away from each other, sticky, itchy, relinquishing dreams. Douglas was seated at the window, his back to them, and he looked out upon a grey sky.

Fatboy was confused by his sense of loss. A protest welled within him, a weak rage that originated with an ache in his balls and seeped into his liver. His sense of being alive carried a bitterness. He stumbled across the impossible: was this all there was, this feeble flicker of sex, the muted lust to kill, to dissolve, to shrink from beginnings? He felt cheated, and hated himself as a cheater. Fatboy felt untouched. He watched Douglas, Douglas's silence, and wondered what it was that he had lost.

"What are you doing in here?" Doreen asked. "Fatboy told you to wait outside."

"He didn't say anything when I came back in."

Fatboy struggled back into his blue jeans, tugged at the zipper of his fly. "I didn't hear you come back in."

"No, you didn't. Guess you were somewhere far away. it was cold in the hall, man. It was too cold to sit out in the hall."

"Jesus, it's cold in here too," Doreen complained. She didn't bother to get dressed again, but slipped under the blanket. Fatboy kept his gaze from her, acutely aware that he didn't know what her body looked like naked, that he barely knew how it felt. She was thin, but somehow boneless. He had the uncomfortable feeling that the sight of her body would somehow disgust him, that her breasts would look like two cold fried eggs, that she would be all gooseflesh and hairless, a plucked chicken. He wanted to leave, to take Douglas with him, to stand at a bar with Douglas, down a few beers and forget that there was such a thing as women, as vampires, as chickens scrawny and plucked, hanging dull-eyed in butchers' windows, their flesh to be eaten, their bones to be cast into the garbage, the marrow within still warm. Women. There was no sense in killing a woman. It was too easy, the thrill was over too soon.

"Douglas," Doreen wheedled, "I want another bag."

"You just did one."

"I want another. I'm not high enough."

"You're high enough. You just don't feel it."

"What does that mean? That doesn't mean anything. What do you mean, I just don't feel it? What good does it do me if I don't feel it? I want to feel it, Douglas. Give me another bag."

Doreen wanted to feel it, Fatboy wanted to forget, Douglas wanted nothing, nada, Fatboy wanted to forget, Doreen wanted to feel it. There was no sense in killing a woman, the thrill was over too soon, she couldn't feel it. Douglas decided to do up another bag himself. He wheeled around to face the bed, drew a bag from his shirt pocket. Doreen watched him with cold eyes, her bleached eyeballs two peeled hardboiled eggs, watched him as he got the stuff ready, watched him shoot it up, watched his face grow lax, his green eyes melt, losing their glow. She watched him with cold eyes and her body grew cold beneath the blanket. "What about me, Douglas? Where's my bag?"

"You don't need it. I told you."

"I do. I need it. Give it to me." She sprang from the bed, and stood in the center of the room, her body goose-fleshed and hairless. For no reason she was angry, willing to hurt, to be hurt. Fatboy felt his stomach twist. He was both hungry and nauseous. Her breasts were small and flat, with soft pale nipples, two cold fried eggs. She was trembling. "Don't play games, Douglas, just give me a bag."

"Put some clothes on, junkie. You'll catch pneumonia running around like that. Put some clothes on. Here's your bag." Doreen stood in the center of the floor, the bag in her hand, not knowing what to do next. She felt even angrier and longed to be more than naked, to have her skin flayed, her flesh flake. A bit more gently Douglas said, "Get dressed, girl. We're going out." She slipped into her dress as Fatboy and Douglas donned their jackets. "Wait for me." Doreen's voice, muffled beneath the tangle of her dress over her head, sounded pleading, pathetic. "Wait for me. I'll go with you."

"We're going out alone. See you later, baby." The two men were out the door, and Doreen, no longer naked, was alone in the center of the room with the bag in her hand. On the stairs going out, Douglas laid his hand on Fatboy's neck. "That was all right, kid. You did okay." They walked down five flights, Douglas's hand lingering, warm on Fatboy's neck. At the door he withdrew his hand, and they moved further apart once out on the street. Fatboy walked with Douglas, knew he was going somewhere, and was willing to go. They stood at a bar and Fatboy downed a couple of beers. Douglas drank tomato juice.

Later that night, after Douglas slapped Fatboy on the back, told him once more, "You did okay. That was all right, kid," and left, going somewhere alone this time, Fatboy walked back down to the pier, to the river. He knelt on the ground to pick up a small black handball. He bounced it once or twice, considered hurling it into the river, then slipped it into his pocket. It was so dark and he had no place to go. He stared into the river, seeing nothing but the reflections of the lights from the land, and wished he could shoot up a bag, maybe a couple of bags. He thought about Douglas, about Douglas killing a man, and about Doreen, about his first bedding of a woman, about Douglas watching him as he lay, unable to move, upon his back while Doreen, lithe and aflame, sucked his seed into her body. It was so dark, it was dark within her body, it was dark within his mind. The river held no mysteries, offered only reflected light. He wished he had no heart, no blood in his veins, no motion in his body.

Fatboy was to see Douglas and Doreen over and over again. He scored for Douglas, selling him Harry's stuff. They all shot a lot of junk together. Never once did they ever mention what happened that afternoon. Never again did Fatboy feel young and stupid enough to ask Douglas what it felt like, what it really felt like, to kill a man. It was as if that afternoon had never happened, as if Fatboy had never known the vampire of Doreen draining his seed from his body. After awhile he began to wonder whether it had really happened at all. It could have been a dream. It should have been a dream. It was crazy, an unwanted memory. It was crazy, unreal, an unreal memory. It had never happened. It couldn't have happened. Fatboy didn't know. Fatboy knew he didn't know. Fatboy stopped trying to know. He wondered, idly, what it was like to kill a man. He knew it couldn't feel like sex, but he somehow forgot what sex felt like. His memories were just memories, something inside, and the world was happening outside, and the two were happening together, but not exactly together, and he couldn't be bothered to understand. He didn't even remember, after all, what he had for breakfast that morning. Or whether he ever ate breakfast at all.

The spring mornings were warm, the evenings still chilly. Summer slammed down on the city, hard, leaving everyone out of breath and dazed with the heat. The little maple was a dried-up heap of twigs, brittle and leafless. Fatboy had known in early spring the maple would die. He didn't know that he would feel so sad when it did. But then, he didn't know that he would ever feel sad, had ever felt sad. He sat on the top step of a brownstone, blocking the doorway. His own death seemed an absurdity, a grossness in a delicate weave. That he would die was possible, that he would die unthinkable. The tree shuddered before his eyes, the wind troubled his hair, and he stopped thinking. Once more, empty of image, he was only seeing a dead tree, a street, an absence of memory.

DRIFT

Everybody seemed to die on Mona. There wasn't any two ways about it. The truth was, if you loved somebody bad enough, that somebody would die and leave you behind, high and dry. And high and dry it was. High cause that was the only way to be when it seemed you had cried once too many a time, and dry because there wasn't a tear left to cry. All the tears had been cried. The next tear to be shed, Mona swore, was going to be at her own funeral, and somebody else was going to be shedding it, cause she was going to be one dry-eyed corpse. And it didn't look like anybody much would shed a tear for Mona, cause she was letting the world know she didn't care for a living soul. She only cared for the dead.

Running over the list of the dead Mona had once cared about, you would have to begin with her grandmother, Grandma O'Hare, on her mother's side. This was the grandmother who lived nearby, down the street to the left, with the white lace curtains starched and ironed fluttering in the open window facing the street. She was a quiet woman, who believed in Jesus Christ and all the saints, who somehow forgot about the Father, who believed in keeping clean and looking good for the neighbors, in always wearing a hat in the street, in the innocence and purity of little children, and especially in giving red and white peppermint balls to good little girls like Mona, who was innocent and pure and kept clean and loved Jesus. She died when Mona was six, leaving nothing behind but a wan waxen face for Mona to kiss and tremble for at the wake. There were candles to light for Grandma O'Hare, and rosaries to tell, and Baby Jesus who cared for the sufferings of little children and would willingly listen to Mona's near-rebellious prayers, but who did not open the grave and bring back Grandma O'Hare and the red and white peppermint balls. That was how you would have to begin, and that was how Mona did begin, when running over the list of the dead.

Aunt Mona, for whom Mona had been named, died next, when Mona herself was nearly ten. Aunt Mona had been the youngest of Grandma O'Hare's children, and Mona's mother's favorite sister.

She was much given to strings of pearls and artificial roses pinned to her flat bosom, to high heel shoes that tapped when she walked and gave a slight curve to her flat and skinny calves, and to laughter. Her laughter was like the perfume she wore, dry and light and persistent, haunting the room she had just left. She married at the age of twenty-four, just when the family had begun to despair of her, and she died five months later, four months pregnant, in a pool of her own vomit in a hospital ward, of an asthma condition she had had since childhood. There was no reason for her to die, the family murmured. If she had stayed at home instead of entering the hospital she would still be alive, for her brothers and sisters, her uncles and aunts, would have sat round the clock with her in her distress. But because she feared for her unborn child, she entered the hospital, where desperate patients in the beds around her called for nurses, for doctors who never came, and Aunt Mona choked in her own vomit, guarded by none but those too weak to leave their own sickbeds. And Mona swore she was never going to have a baby, to die unloved in a hospital bed, that she had rather be a nun and be bride to Jesus, who fathered no children and caused no one to die.

But Mona was not to become a nun, for her mother died when Mona was thirteen, just at the age, Mona later realized, when a girl needed a mother most. Her mother's death Mona found ludicrous, for she had just begun to hate her, to wish that she would die, and then she died, hit by a car in full view of Mona, in front of her own house. It was so funny, Mona decided, that she began to laugh and laugh, and only stopped laughing when they, the neighbors, the family, the policemen at the scene of the accident, decided to bring Mona to the hospital to treat her for shock. Dreading the hospital, where they let people die, the girl stopped laughing, and averted her face from the sight of her mother, dressed for shopping in her black broadcloth coat, with the little fox fur tight about her neck, her eyes as glazed and alert as they stared at the sun as the glass eyes set in the head of the little dead fox. She had to avert her eyes, she knew, or she would laugh again, laugh at the two sets of eyes unblinking in the sun's glare, at the glimpse of rolled stocking or wasted thighs, never before exposed to light, at the neat practical shoes, the left one with a hole in the ball of the sole, at the fox fur and the drying blood foxcolored upon the ground.

There was nothing to laugh at in death, Mona told herself, and suddenly sober she leaped into the arms of her two brothers, who shielded her from hospitals, from laughter, from foxfur and staring eyes. There was strength in those arms, and the motherless girl drew solace from them for a while, even though they were to lead to other solacing arms, broad and muscled, and she was never to become a nun, not without a mother's arms to shelter her. But that was later. She was only thirteen, after all, and her brothers were brawlers and strong.

The arms of the two brawling brothers seemed to reach out to embrace death, for one died a soldier somewhere in Asia in a war that was not called a war, but for whatever words the government or the army were to call it, and they called it a police action, he died a soldier in a war, and the tattoo on his arm, the arm blown off as he died, read For God and Country. The other brother died of an overdose of heroin, and his arms were as permanently marked as his tattooed brother's were, the veins blackened and collapsed, the needle still in his vein when he was found, the blood dry on his forearm the color of foxfur.

And so it seemed to Mona that all the people she had ever loved were dead and gone. There were left of course her father, but he was small and potbellied and bitter and bullying, and when he drank too much, which seemed to be more and more often, he cried, and Mona detested him in everything he did, in his job, for he was a common laborer, carrying bricks in wheelbarrows to men who were more skilled than he, in his taste in alcohol, for he preferred beer to whiskey and bought the cheapest of piss-pale brands, and in his bullying, which was feeble and mean, not even dignified by violent rage. He would sit at the kitchen table and carp, criticizing Mona's dress and behavior, in language no more imaginative than "You're a shit, that's what you are. A little whore," which he pronounced *hoo-er.* "If your mother was alive to see you she would drop dead in her tracks, you shit."

Also there were her remaining brothers and sisters, two boys and three girls, but they were all younger than her and seemed forever to have little colds, with perpetual running noses and earaches that sent screams into the night, disturbing her beauty sleep. The burden of the housework fell on her, but she managed to shrug it off, and thus her brothers and sisters became an eyesore, an embarrassment, always dressed in dirty unpressed clothes, cadging afternoon snacks from the neighbors, and getting into one kind of trouble after another.

No, there was no one left to love, and it was a risk loving the living anyway, it seemed a curse put on them to make them die. Her last bit of love seemed lost with the baby who died at birth, the firstborn of a pair of twins, and as she cried for the one child she fretted with resentment for the other, the living one, the infant girl who ate up her time, for Mona was just turned nineteen, and she felt she had very little time, that somehow all the light bright years, the dazzle of youth with all the glow and excitement and beauty and promise, were being drained by the child at her breast the way her breasts were being drained of milk, leaving them flat and wrinkled and prematurely aged.

But all this was so much later, after her brothers had died and she had wondered at the mysteries of their deaths, of the need of man for war, the need of junkies for dope. The last bit of life left to her, the baby nursing at her breast, had been born a dope addict itself and had nearly died, had kicked in the hospital and began to take in dope again in mother's milk the same day the mother had come home to begin life anew, leaving death behind in a hospital morgue. So much later, long after her brother had died of heroin and she had sought out his friends to discover what had really happened and why, and how in the arms of boys her brother's age she had found a few attempts at answers, had found caresses and sex and needle marks and needles shared. It was for friendship he had died, they seemed to say. For love, for sharing, for being together with people who really understood each other, understood need, understood want. War they couldn't explain, for they were not warriors. If they took life they took it as assassins, secretly, alone, regretfully, in the dark. War could not lure them, violence for them was quick and rarely necessary, for they preferred peace and solitude and the distant companionship of their kind. And Mona, so familiar with death and so tired of crying, found that she was their kind. And in living from now to so much later, she found a little flutter of loving, a brush of sensuality, a lot of quiet, an answer, a way, a pregnancy, a birth, an end to dying.

And so when the list was exhausted, and the catechism of names was ended, Mona found there was really no one to blame for death. She couldn't blame God, for when she was fifteen she couldn't keep on confessing while remaining unrepentant, and if she couldn't confess and be absolved she couldn't take communion, and if she couldn't take communion she couldn't go to church because everyone would see her in a state of sin, unwilling to go and sin no more, and besides she just didn't feel like going to church anyhow, and if she couldn't go to church she couldn't live with it if she kept on believing in God, and if she couldn't believe in Him she couldn't blame Him at all. And all that was just fine with Mona. God must get tired of being blamed for everything all the time, she thought with a facial quirk that used to be a smile, God would appreciate not being believed in.

And she couldn't blame luck. Luck wasn't anybody anyhow, although an old gambler she knew, a man sporting a pencil mustache of all things and an ancient green fedora, always referred to luck as Lady Luck, but Mona knew he was just doing that because he had to do something about being such a badluck gambler, that he needed luck to be a lady because the ladies just weren't any good at all, they were as fickle as luck herself. Mona knew that luck wasn't anybody, there was no blaming luck.

There was no blaming doctors and nurses who weren't there, or Baby Jesus, or the inefficacy of prayer, or drivers who got their bumpers bloody, or soldiers who were dying even as they killed or needles innocent of intent or pushers or strangling umbilical cords or luck or God. There was no blaming anybody. If Mona blamed anybody for her sorrows and her tears, she blamed the dead. It was the dead she wept for, the dead she grieved for. The living couldn't hurt her at all. It was the dead she blamed, the dead ridiculous in their foxfurs, their perfume unable to mask the choking odor of vomit, their tattoos, their waxen serenity, their artificial repose. It was the dead who made life and the living ludicrous, by exposing their thighs to the eyes of those unable to lust for rolled stockings on dead meat, by staring open-eyed into the sun without blinking or by never having seen the light of day, by being blown to pieces, by being dead where they had once been alive, and everything made useless, their hopes and fantasies endowed with a shade more eternity than they ever were, lingering to remind the living that their own hopes and fantasies were worth more than their sordid little realities. So Mona remained dry-eyed, her shallow dry laugh replacing tears. She was letting the world know she didn't care for a living soul. She only cared for the dead; and in the name of dry justice she only blamed the dead.

This is not to say that Mona was tough. She quivered constantly against the next moment, although her eyes were shrewd and her voice was sharp, she awaited each blast of winter with all the aplomb of an aspen. Somehow she was aware, but only vaguely, that her vision of life was shadowy, oblique; that she had lived but couldn't quite tell how, that all the years that had led to the fragment of now she felt suddenly isolated within were so blurred that her memories might well be fiction, that she herself might well be an artist's quick sketch, imperfectly drawn and tossed aside. Even those remembrances of deaths, seemingly so finely etched, so careless of time spent and gone in their clarity, were reduced to brilliant miniatures, stereopticons of the soul, essentially toys.

And Mona herself was then no more than a marshmallow, a piece of fluff, a speck of dust. At times like these Mona would hurl herself away from all contact with the artifacts of her life, would abandon baby and apartment and dirty dishes incessantly piled in the sink, and would walk desperately through streets unremarkable, unremarked, until she would catch up with herself, panting, in front of some store window, some playground, some unfamiliar corner where life announced itself as being, without giving a damn for Mona's acknowledgment or choice. The sharpness of sound, traffic noises, human voices, or the disquiet of night stillness, would awaken an inner echo of a baby crying, moaning, perhaps strangling on its bedclothes, and Mona would rush home, to lock herself again within familiar walls, listening to the maddening rhythm of life breathing, sharing space with her. Grudgingly, Mona loved her baby. She found it unbearable that the child loved her too.

Somehow the vagueness condensed, and in the shadow world she lived in, people with contacts, dealers, marks, shopkeepers with a worried eye on the overhead mirror, cops, three friends appeared like landmarks, their names as musical as foghorns sounding on a starless night. Douglas, Freddie, Doreen. Douglas, who talked about things people had to listen to, Freddie, who remembered death with more chilling finality than Mona, though he never talked, and Doreen, Douglas's woman.

There is a drift that is steady and slow, a definite tide that binds years together, and thus the four, the two couples, man and woman repeated twice for good measure, drifted together. Mona and Doreen looked alike, too thin and sharp, everything in their faces washed out but for glowing feline eyes, predatory and quick. Mona knew Doreen without having to answer questions, recognized her in her undefined calf muscles, the triangular bones of her face, the limpness of her hair. When they did talk their conversation was trite, gossipy and impressionistic, but full of genuine pleasure. The form was imitative, the undercurrent true.

Doreen was with Douglas because she was persistent, had been around for years, had seized her moment and extended it into habit. Douglas accepted her good-humoredly, without question; a flightless bird, a rare mudgrubber. As for Douglas, his plumage shimmered, bedazzled; his iridescence became mirror-like, so that as his friends came to know themselves better, Douglas disappeared. Doreen hung on his arm, chattering brightly, Douglas was silent save for his eyes. He shone, she was eclipsed, she loved him, he cared for her, she whored for his habit, he lived with her habit. They were a happy couple.

Freddie was silent in several languages. Dark skinned, pockmarked, kinky-haired, he considered himself ugly and knew he was sexually magnetic. He spoke Spanish, also Ladino, German, also Yiddish, and could quote and translate the Latin Mass with light irony. He was halting in Hebrew and Arabic, and claimed to be a Canadian national when pressed. He spoke a vernacular, ungrammatical American, at rare excited moments oddly accented. He preserved his air of mystery as one would cherish a family heirloom, and shrank from Douglas's metaphysics at the same time that he inexorably sought his company. He had met Mona in the island of concrete playground surrounded by traffic to which she brought her daughter; she also scored there, for the wooden-slatted benches were lined with junkies, some buying, some selling. Mona was junk-sick, she was waiting for a usually reliable friend to come back after giving him ten dollars for her and ten for him, and she had just belted Karen when the child came running to her in tears, her knee bloody. Freddie shot forward with the action of a sprung switchblade and slapped Mona with the same vehemence with which she had struck her child. He then lifted the little girl in his arms and turning to the stunned mother, growled, "C'mon, junkie, I've got enough stuff in my pocket to kill you and ten of your friends." She followed him, he asked where she lived, she brought him home with her and he never left. He didn't care for Mona much but he liked her kid. He hinted at having loved a child who resembled Karen, a child who had died, but when or where, whether she was daughter or sister, he never said. It was good for Mona. She always had almost enough junk.. Freddie was a thief of professional caliber, with no compunctions, and not much dedication to his habit. To him it was just a habit, not a faith.

They had drifted with death and were tied together by death. Death for them was remembered, or dreaded, or known, a small twisted lump lodged in consciousness that could not be dislodged save for the jar of the needle, the smoothing out of awareness that heroin brought. Yet that was not really all there was to it. Even with the heroin there existed the jangle of death, perhaps because of it. And even if there were not that weighty obsession with finality, they would have been heroin addicts. They were heroin addicts because they used heroin, in the final analysis. Any other reason offered was pure intellectualizing, the play of minds in love with the hypothesis, the closed system in which all truths held, reality examined in candlelight, under the aegis of romance. And in their lyrical science was the smell of death.

It is easier to tell of these four the who and what they thought they were than to tell of their actions, for they rarely acted. They sought a state of suspended animation, in which all there was to live was already lived, and all the future a mist, a limbo that served in lieu of nothing. If nothing was what they wanted, it was not, however, what they had. To attain nothing involves volition, action, and their wills were suspended, their actions narrowing circles spiraling to a fixed point, exceedingly limited, where action would be forced. They did not know they were circling toward action, but they sensed it. The spur of action was death.

Douglas perhaps was the only one who realized that they were only alive when death spoke. His eyes were green, and he viewed the world through a green lens, a world that quivered with an insistent duality of growth and rot. Overwhelmed by the shimmering play of cyclic motion, the wild and patterned dance of birth and being and death, Douglas retreated to a point within himself, seeking finality, an absolute, an infinity. But within or without, he found only the range of greens, the overview, the color of thought. Unable to find answers, he offered an answer. He became for himself the answer, and thus to himself he became for everyone an answer. He gave himself as sacrifice, delivering his will to the wills of others, playing any role asked of him. If an addict was needed by a pusher, then he would become that addict. He would be addict, dealer, target, lover, pimp. If a junkie was desperate for junk and needed to burn another junkie for his own need, then Douglas allowed himself to be burned, to be the patsy, the fall guy, the sucker. If that same junkie needed a good connection, then Douglas would be streetwise. For all the patron saints and Our Ladies Of he dedicated himself to the closed system of junk. He did not choose it nor was it thrust upon him; it happened. Nothing else was to happen. The system yawned and swallowed: Jonah inside the whale.

Douglas saw the drift. He had the facility for seeing beneath the mask of flesh the grinning deaths-head beneath, of seeing that same skull dissolved into dust, the same dust that first caught the spark that was first cosmos, then life, that was death. It was a fragment of a vision he kept secret within himself, drifting with his fellow drifters, the glowing green of eyes within his skull noncommittal as they touched other eyes alive and trapped within other skulls. Yet others, like Mona, like Doreen, like Freddie, saw something in that impassive gaze. Street sphinx, he satisfied their neonate cry for answers with riddles.

During a panic, a scarcity of heroin, Mona ran to Douglas, found him and Doreen as sick as she was.

"Douglas," Mona tensed attenuated and burning with dry fire, "You gotta do something."

"I tried. There's nothing to do."

"But I can't stand it. I'll die. I'll go crazy. Please, Douglas, for the love of God, do something, find something."

She believed she would die, would go insane. She believed it. And it was true. Like all men and women, she would go insane, she would die, she would go insane, she would die.

"Where's Freddie?" Douglas asked.

"Home with the kid." Mona began to cry.

"Me and Freddie, we'll do something."

They doctored themselves as best they could with kaopectate and antihistamines. "It's not just the sickness, Douglas. You understand. It's not just the sickness. I can be sick, Douglas. I can be sick all right. I feel like I'm going crazy. It feels like I'm dying. I don't want to die."

Douglas promised he would do something. Leaving Doreen and Mona together, he went to find Freddie. Both Freddie and the kid were gone.

During a panic, drugstores in a heroin-dry city, particularly in junkie neighborhoods, take extraordinary precautions. The drugstores in Douglas's area locked their doors, admitting only known customers, the aged, or people obviously respectable or in trouble. Douglas needed Freddie, needed Mona's kid Karen in order to take off a drugstore. He began to search the streets, methodically checking every known place where Freddie, where any junk-sick addict, might be found. He had no luck. After two hours, weakened and nauseous, he went home. He found Freddie in his place, engaged in a shouting match with Mona. Mona seemed to be doing most of the shouting.

"I tell you to watch the kid, you watch the kid. You don't leave her alone." Mona was too sick to be purple-faced with rage, but her eyes bulged. Douglas's eyes flinched away from the green tinge to her face.

"You leave her alone plenty of times, bitch. Don't put your shit on me." Freddie, normally very contained, had his hands balled into fists, showed the broken stumps of his front teeth in a snarl. "Anyway, I didn't leave her alone. I left her with Mrs. Gomez."

"You're lying!" Mona raved. "You're lying, you're no good, you're lying. Mrs. Gomez would never watch her. She hates me. I even offered to pay her, pay her good, and she would never watch her for me."

"That's because you're a junkie, bitch, you're a junkie and a whore. That's why she won't watch her for you."

"And you're not a junkie, huh? What do you think you are, faggot? You're a junkie too."

"Yeah, but she don't know that. I don't scream it all over the neighborhood the way you do. Anyway, I told her I was going to look for you, that you left me with the kid and that I had to go to work, that you were up to no good and when I found you I was going to break your ass. Which I might just do, bitch, if you don't shut your mouth."

"You told her that? She'll watch the kid for you but not for me, right? I'll show you. I'll show both of you. I'll show all of you." Mona flung herself at Freddie, her hands flying, woman-fashion, straight for his eyes, her nails, polished red, glinting with the female promise of blood. Freddie grappled her, nails and teeth and kicking feet, crushed her in his arms, threw her to the floor, and kicked her, harder than usual. The pain was sobering. She stopped screaming, stopped crying, and began to moan.

"Where's Doreen?" Douglas asked.

"I gave her some money," Freddie mumbled, rubbing sweat from his forehead with the base of his palm. "She said she had this barbiturate connection."

"Jesus," Douglas said softly. "I know who you mean. He's no good. I hope she doesn't get hurt. He'd just as soon take her off for the money as sell to her. Not that the money's gonna do him any good. There's no shit anywhere in this whole world, I could swear to that."

"Yeah, well," Freddie answered, not caring, "she didn't seem too worried."

"She shoulda waited for me. I woulda got it. Why didn't you go with her?"

"This bitch here. Had a lot of screaming to do. Who doesn't like being sick. The only one in the world. Pig." Freddie spat at her, landing a blob of sputum on her leg. She didn't move. Her moans stopped.

"Come on, man. We got a job to do."

"What kind of job?" Freddie asked.

"Tell you later. Let's go."

"I wanna wait for Doreen to come back. I need something, Douglas. I need a little something."

Mona sat up, her face drained of hate, panic in her eyes. "You gonna leave me alone?"

Douglas smiled at her. "Doreen'll be back soon."

"Maybe. What if something happens to her?" Mona began twisting the hem of her skirt. She wiped off the spit from her leg with it.

"Then you'll be alone for a little while. Don't sweat it."

"Don't tell me not to sweat it," Mona snapped. "I'm sweating it."

"So are we all," Douglas said. He and Freddie left. Mona dragged herself to the toilet, leaned over it. Her stomach empty, she retched dry for ten shattering minutes, almost wishing she were dead.

In the street, Freddie turned to Douglas, his eyebrows arching. "What's the job?"

"Drugstore," Douglas answered.

"No good, man. Everything's too tight."

"Not the way I got it planned," Douglas replied. We gotta pick up the kid first."

"Karen?"

"Karen. We can't score without the kid."

Douglas and Freddie turned left at the corner, avoiding the playground full of sick, desperately hopeful junkies, and walked the four flights up to Mrs. Gomez, where they picked up the kid, leaving behind the smell of drying diapers, ammonia, and plantains frying in oil, and the sound of a baby crying, a radio announcer extolling the virtues of a credit furniture store in idiomatic Spanish, and the growl and scuffle of two little boys, one brain damaged and the other hare-lipped, fighting in front of a broken television set. Karen was delighted with her freedom, with the two grimly silent men who promised her a walk in the street, under a grey sun.

On a side street of rooming houses and transient hotels and small businesses was a tiny drugstore, a shop that once provided perhaps the only, certainly the cheapest, medical care to a neighborhood of immigrant families. The aged proprietor, who had never been able to fulfill his dream of being a doctor, had practiced medicine nevertheless, dispensing drugs to people unable to afford a doctor, arranging abortions for unmarried young girls and mothers who had not menstruated in ten years, so closely spaced were their children. The desperate families had long been replaced by transients whose medical needs were fulfilled at the liquor store or by local pushers, and the new families who lived along the broad avenues preferred the chain stores, which sold more cosmetics and patent medicines than they fulfilled prescriptions. The little drugstore was going out of business, slowly, for the last seven years. The old man was all alone in his store. He kept the front door locked, opening only to his few known customers. This was the store Douglas and Freddie had decided would be the easiest to take off. Their only worry was that someone else would get there first.

A few doors away from the drugstore Freddie slapped Karen on the right ear, hard. Douglas carried her screaming to the store, rang the buzzer. The old man peered through the glass. Freddie gesticulated wildly at the kid, pointing to her ear, to his ear, his face a grimace of anxiety. The old man nodded, unbolted the door, and let them come in, locking the door behind them. Douglas set Karen down on a wooden chair next to a display case. Karen, who was usually warned to shut up or she'd get it if she cried, took advantage of the sympathy and attention she was getting, and delightedly howled her pain. Freddie yelled in the old man's ear, "She's got an earache. I don't know a doctor. We just moved in."

The druggist bent over Karen, reached into his pocket, drew out a sucking candy, and gave it to her. As she popped it into her mouth the druggist pushed her hair away from her ear. Douglas grabbed the man from behind and wrestled him towards the back of the store, away from the window with its view of the street. Freddie held a knife to the man's belly, murmuring a soft apology as he did so. Karen sucked her candy.

"Sorry, fella, but you're gonna let us into the back, and no trouble." The old man nodded quickly. He was retiring, he had nothing more to lose. He knew junkies. "Key's in my jacket pocket," he rasped, not knowing why he was whispering. Douglas dipped into the pocket, found the key.

"You got a dog in there, man, you better call him off, or I'll rip your guts out," Freddie said, also whispering. The old man nodded, quicker, harder. "No dog, no dog. I'm afraid of dogs."

"All right, all right," Douglas snapped, dragging him along to the back. Once in the back room Freddie quickly went for whatever he recognized, morphine pills, opium in solution, paregoric, barbiturates, prescription disposable syringes, Darvons, Demerols, tranquilizers, neomorphine. He searched, unsuccessfully, for methadone. The old man didn't stock it, wouldn't stock it. "Over there, baby," Douglas would suggest, as Freddie ran through the stock. "Okay, okay, you got it all," Douglas finally said.

"What about him?" Freddie asked.

"Tie him up."

"There's nothing around."

Douglas searched the room with his eyes. There was nothing, no parcels tied with cord, nothing. The old man had, after all, been going out of business for a long time. "Lock him in here," Douglas suggested.

"No good. The back door, right over there."

Douglas saw Freddie's knife hand twitch. "Uh uh," he frowned. Freddie dashed for the front, came back with the display mortar and pestle in his hand. He lifted the metal pestle, the old man cringed, cried out, and collapsed in Douglas's arms as the pestle struck once, twice, thrice. Douglas dropped the man, sprang away from the gushing blood.

"You're just lucky I'm not full of blood, man," Douglas snapped.

They crammed bottles and jars into their pockets, ran for the front, grabbed Karen's hand, and ran out the door. Once in the street they slowed, crossed the street, tugging Karen along as she dawdled, looking at things, just things, anything, everything in sight. Once around the corner the two men relaxed somewhat. If no one spotted them coming out, then they were safe. They rounded one more corner and headed back to Douglas's place, to Mona and Doreen.

The table on which Freddie and Douglas dumped their pocketful of drugs was in front of an uncurtained window. Douglas stood by the window, shielding the spill of drugs and syringes from Mona's grasping hands with his body. He searched the street below for Doreen, expecting to see her emerge from between two parked cars, to round a corner, to dart out from a storefront, her raincoat collar turned up against the wind, against the faint rain that was just beginning to fall. He saw the street in all that sharp detail that a grey day brings out, the green lettering of A. Vitale and Son intense on the orange awning of the greengrocer, the wet brown fur of an elderly woman's coat collar bedraggled in a mist of raindrops, the glint of rust on a twisted can forgotten at the curb. He didn't see any sign of Doreen. He turned toward the room. Mona was standing before him, saliva coating the dullness of her grey-tinged teeth. Freddie was slumped against a wall, his eyes vacant.

"We divide this four ways," Douglas said.

"There's only three of us here," Mona wailed.

"Doreen gets her share or me and Freddie will divide it two ways."

Mona measured her chances against the green of Douglas's eyes. He looked mad to her. She gave in. "Have it your way."

Douglas began to split the pile into four smaller piles. Mona watched in agony, wanting to run with her first few pills, her first needle, to boil down and shoot up before life ended suddenly, cheating her out of one last high, before an airplane crashed into the building, before the police came, before the bomb fell, before her heart gave up in disgust. Yet she knew she couldn't leave, couldn't trust Douglas and Freddie any more than she could trust life, couldn't let them pocket a few extra pills that by rights, because fair was fair, belonged to her. They had probably pocketed enough already. When the distribution was complete, Mona sprang with her booty for the bed. There was no stove in the apartment, and the hotplate was broken, so she began the laborious process of cooking down her supply of morphine over a book of matches. Freddie and Douglas, after a long look at each other, began to do the same. Karen prowled the apartment restlessly, finally settling down in the closet amid Doreen's collection of high heeled shoes. After the three shot up, they lay silently back on the bed, waiting without worry for Doreen. She showed two hours later, stoned, and woke Karen up when she kicked her shoes off into the closet.

"What are you high on?" Mona asked jealously.

"Dope." Doreen giggled inanely, the old-fashioned word lying limp from her tongue, floating on the air before her. "I am high on the real stuff. Wanna buy some?"

"Where'd you get it?" Douglas asked.

"It's a long story. Brooklyn. What you high on?"

"Morphine for starts," Freddie said. "We got all kinds of pills and goodies."

"Save it for a rainy day," Doreen purred. "Here's your money back. I didn't get the downs. Very bad news scene. Now, who wants to buy some scag?"

Drift. They were high, they would continue to get high. The old man lingered for a few days before dying, the real thing, upon clean white sheets that the nurse's aide had just slipped under his unconscious form. His store died too, to be replaced by another liquor store a month later. Douglas and Doreen and Mona and Freddie never found out that he died. They wouldn't have cared. Death comes, that they knew, death has a claim and must be fulfilled. Doreen didn't think about death, because she was afraid of it, and didn't like to be afraid, and didn't like to think. Douglas didn't think about death, because he had already thought about it, once. That once remained, a mist of green that colored everything life-colored, death-colored. Thinking was now, always. Freddie didn't think about death, because he had already died, already been buried, and killed for resurrection, a resurrection that never came. And Mona, pale Mona, burdened with her child, didn't think about death because she knew that to think about death was to force death's hand, to force death to think about you. Mona, needle-sharp, rested her hand upon Karen's head, and the points of her red nails dug into the child's head. The child shrugged the hand away. The hand fell listlessly into Mona's lap. It didn't seem like Mona's hand. It could have been anyone's hand, thought Mona, a loveless hand that became a claw when it rested on the tangled hair of a small child. Although the hand was turned palm down, Mona could see in her secret vision the scabs upon her wrist. She was shooting in her wrist now, the veins in the crook of her elbow were too collapsed to admit another assault from a needle.

IX. CRY WOLF

Douglas, movie maker, turned his green eyes inward, and found no image. Thus his movie began without image, without light, but with a sound of worship and hunger, a vibration of being that was a river, a river of sound that was blood, that was thought, an ocean of thought that crashed salty upon barren rock. The sound was to remain, a whisper, an echo, a hum to underscore the motion of action revealed from its first non-image, void, to an arbitrary end. This is my movie, this is my consciousness, these are my senses creating first chaos, then pattern, upon the perfection of mind emerging from void.

Because it is my movie I am prophet, I am seer, and for an instant that seems not ever to have had existence, I see my movie in full, the serpent biting his own tail. Douglas, movie maker, turned his green eyes outward.

A montage of Gothic vaulting, of grey membrane tinged pink with an underlayer of blood, the vibration of sound all encompassing, heartbeat! blinding light a deluge of rainbow, glowing whitely. Image out of focus, meaninglessness of visions in frowned juxtaposition, the heartbeat reduced to inner vibration, barely translated into the possibility of sound. My birth sequence, granted unlimited poetic license. Freedom to create claimed.

Freedom to create. Flashback. Clouds of cosmic dust, explosions of energy, timeless starry night, carbon compounds organic the zombies of space. Pre-life. Law. The electrons resolve themselves into dance, negative densities, agglomeration, gravity. Law. Flashback. Pre-time.

A movie without image, without sound. A mind without consciousness, pre-sensation. God and all the angels, a heavenly host. Numbers and the word.

Douglas, movie maker, defined the limits of freedom. Choice. He panned the street, the rows of brownstones, the grain of stone, the play of reflected light and hollow darkness, windows closed, windows open.

Five doors painted green, two doors painted red, three doors painted green, one door painted grey, one door painted green, one door painted red, four doors painted green, two doors painted brown, three doors painted green, one door painted blue, a vacant lot, weed-grown and filled with debris, one door painted blue, one door painted green, six doors painted brown, one door painted blue, one door painted orange, four doors painted yellow. Blues electric, blues pale, greys pearl and ashen and dove, browns earthen and chocolate and muddy, reds rust and lipstick, greens grassy, greens mossy, yellow ocher, yellow buttery, colors intense and colors faded. Animal life. Cats, people, pigeons, sparrows, dogs. Traffic. The other side of the street, storefronts, a drugstore selling trusses and perfumes, a greengrocer's, a self- service shoe store cut-rate, a supermarket, a luncheonette, a miracle of nothing in extremes calling itself Superette, a butcher shop featuring hog maw, pig's feet, spare ribs, and chitterlings cleaned and ready to cook, chickens whole and cut up small southern fry style. . . . Cut to traffic on a two-way street, a green bus pulling to a stop, its front door opening, the green of Douglas's eyes resting on an exact change only sign, coins dropping through a metal slot. Cut to streets seen in motion, a blur of color, a loss of detail. Douglas, movie maker, grew bored with art.

It is only my eyes, my ears, my nose, my tongue, my skin, my translations, my awareness. It is only myself. How lonely it is to be only me, only Douglas, only a name picked by other boundaries of flesh with names picked by other boundaries of flesh. The cosmos did not resolve itself, the boundaries did not dissolve into unity, reality and illusion were two words as arbitrary in application as in syllabification and sound.

Douglas, suddenly carsick, nauseated with motion, got off the bus, stood on a street corner, disoriented, unable to relate himself to time and space, not knowing where to go. Douglas, movie maker, did not know how to stop the movie in his head. A flow of energy tried to burst forth from the boundaries of flesh; thwarted, it curled in the pit of his stomach, shrank into itself, uncoiled, retreated, flexed, vibrated.

Douglas felt weak. I am sick. Oh god, I am oh Douglas you are oh I am sick. Pasty-faced, with glazed eyes and churning stomach, Douglas grew roots, penetrated cement, became a statue on a street corner.

The city, its motion, its life, dissolved, and Douglas was a sense of permanence, a direction unto himself, with no place to go and nothing to do.

Sudden flow of adrenaline. At some distance, but heading his way, a blue uniform encasing a machine of flesh and blood, nightstick, holster, gun. Douglas began to walk, purposefully, with somewhere to go.

I have no place to go. I have nothing to do. I do not know who I am. Douglas, movie maker, ripped at his eye-gems, tore them from their sockets, tossed them onto the street where they gazed uncomprehending at his blind rage. Blindness was not enough. In a fury he scrabbled at his bony sockets with his fingernails, spent months digging through his skull until his brain gleamed naked, a brain white and pure, quivering as air rushed over its convolutions, spilling onto the sidewalk, a delicate jelly. No use. Inside his skull another brain, mirror image of the coiled whiteness lying on the cement next to his emerald eyes, formed itself anew. The bone of his eye sockets closed over his cranial cavity, new eyes, green and sighted, grew in his head. Again he plucked out his eyes, again they reformed. He felt no truth of sex. Oedipus did not castrate himself, for all his motherfucking.

There was no sense of sin in his balls, in his brain, but his eyes offended him. The world assaulted him through his eyes, made itself a movie for his torment and delight. After a restful sleep comes awakening. Douglas walked through the park. Even in its deepest gullies, sheltered by its loftiest trees, the spires of the buildings that surrounded the park still pierced the skies. The city could still be seen.

Gasoline fumes could still be smelled, traffic noises still heard. The sky above was sorrowful blue, the clouds mothersoft and white, the sun a glorious firewheel. Here were things as they had been, not reeking of man's inventiveness; a bird in sudden flight, lacework of leaves and sky, trees and moss and earth. Douglas headed for the wildest, loneliest part of the park. Here the underbrush was lush and alive with small unseen creatures, the trees were tall and smooth-barked. Here he could hear birdsong. He sat on a rock beneath a tree.

Opposite from Douglas another rock bore a brass plate, tarnished with verdigris, engraved with information about the geological history of the rock. Faggots cruised along the flagstone walk. A mother with four young dirty-faced children asked directions of Douglas. How do I go from here to there. I don't know. I don't think I'll ever get home myself, lady. God bless your little children. An airplane passed overhead, making airplane noises. A sage who had given all away and had gone to live in the wilderness was asked whether or not he regretted the loss of his riches.

Before I came to live here, he answered, I had no riches, but now oh! the miracle of the cherry trees in full blossom. Douglas emptied his pockets, handed his collection of nickels and dimes to the four children.

He would have to walk home. The young mother was afraid of him. He could smell her fear. The tallest of the children, a girl with a wild look to her eyes that even in prepubescence was rich with sexuality, thanked him. As they walked away she turned and blew him a kiss. Her mother yanked her by the arm, hurried faster away, away from the handsome madman who sat on a rock, a man with no place to go, nothing to do, a man who did not know who he was. There were no cherry trees in full blossom to be seen, but every other tree was crowned with the flowers of masonry, of city rooftops. Again Douglas felt wounded in his eyes, felt the green of foliage and the green of his eyeballs torn by the fruits of the labor of men. Homosexuals with the glittering eyes of wolves, cruising, regarded him as meat, dismembered him with the pathos of their desires. He longed to escape from people, from men, from the works of men. He longed to be alone, an eremite upon a mountain peak. He refused to acknowledge that he too was a man. He found too strong a demarcation between the universe and humankind, between the blooming of the cherry trees and the efflorescence of human action. He lay upon the ground with his head against the rock and slept.

Douglas dreamed that he was Jesus Christ.

Drift. The Three Fates sought Douglas, to disabuse him of his illusions, to deny him his dreams. In his sleep Douglas's blood flowed with the same rhythm of the rivers that wound through the city, and the rhythm of the waters flowed with the bloodstreams of three women who in their anonymous lives played with the city as if it were a spangled, sullied toy.

They were called to Douglas, blood to blood, and to Douglas they came.

Sister Calliope shuffled through Times Square, a small squat woman huddled in a soiled and faded shawl, her feet bulging through worn-out shoes. She wore the remains of a feathered hat, and dragged a torn and well-stuffed shopping bag. She was thousands of unknown faces each day, Times Square faces limned with the motley of human misery, a tawdry catalogue of faces marked drug addiction, alcoholism, common prostitution, chronic gambling and chronic losing, petty larceny, the knowledge of every con game, each face stamped with the fear of ending, the sordid and feeble struggle with the shadow of death. The masks of faces advertised their sins against self in gaudy paints or tints of bleak ash, fixed in constipated gaiety or stylized strength, and Sister Calliope no longer had the fortitude to read each one. There were too many, and their thoughts were universally furtive and desperate. She nervously adjusted her violet-tinged sunglasses and avoided meeting the many hollow eyes surrounding her as she trudged the derelict streets.

Pavement smacked against the thin soles of her shoes. Buildings jutted into the sunless, starless sky. Lights of many colors twinkled the obscene messages of greasy food and greasy sex. Noise was as chronic as the overcrowding. The temples were locked against the homeless and the wanting, while screaming their neon salvation next to the storefronts filled with dollar ties and watches that would never work.

Sister Calliope was not welcome in the towering temples of the city's gods. Her oracle was chained to silence; should she preach it would be in the bowels of Bellevue Hospital with the other indiscreet visionaries and seers. Sister Calliope, sagging with the concentrated soul of centuries, clutched her shawl tighter about her shoulders and searched for home. Her blood sang with a calling. She headed for the park, to consult with the man who dreamed he was Jesus Christ.

Farms once covered Brooklyn, and before them the forests and meadows were the hunting grounds of the Canarsie Indians, and before them the animals preyed upon each other. Eohippus died stillborn here, and here the glaciers stopped. Three million people made their home in Brooklyn while Douglas slept beneath a downy-barked tree in Central Park. Many dwelt stacked upon each other, and the weight of their lives crushes the past. There are many women of thirty-five years of age or thereabouts in Brooklyn, wide-hipped and anonymous, dams of three or six or ten or more whelps, transplanted from the different Europes of Scandinavia and the Mediterranean and the Balkans, from the British Isles, from Mediterranean Africa and the Near East, from the different tropics, India, the Caribbean, Central and South Africa, Malaysia, the Far East, Central and South Americas. There are even North American Indians still living in Brooklyn. There are all these mothers, screaming from tenement windows in a cacophony of accents for their wandering pups to come home. They trail from store to store with baby carriages and strollers and shopping carts, dragging armloads of laundry and balking toddlers, littering the sidewalk with children, polluting the land with the realization of their fertility. They are noisy and strong and procreative, as will be their daughters and their daughters' daughters.

One of these women felt her blood sing.

Sister Esta mopped her brow with her forearm, and continued ironing without breaking rhythm. Three starched ruffled pink dresses hung on hangers from the doorknob of the hall closet, and six white shirts were neatly laid out on the folding cot that filled the tiny hall. She finished ironing the flat pieces, sheets, pillowcases, handkerchiefs, and hair ribbons, set the iron to rest on the back of the stove where her younger children couldn't reach, collapsed the ironing board and returned it to the hall closet with its pomander and secrecy. She opened a can of grape soda and poured the soda into a smoky green tumbler, then slumped into a kitchen chair, sighing. It was ten degrees hotter in the cramped kitchen on the fifth floor right under the roof than it was in the streets.

The diviners of old rested their eyes on a tangle of trees, ferns, and moss, listened to the blended music of birdcall and the language of springs welling from hidden lips cleft in the many mysteries of the earth. Shafts of sunlight forced their way through thick boughs to dapple with a golden radiance the noon darkness of lush forests and sparkled on the prisms of glacial lakes. Sister Esta gazed out her windows into a courtyard, seeing staring windows with broken panes and scattered shades, fire escapes cluttered with mops and buckets and area rugs airing, relieved only by the bitter lost beauty of an isolated houseplant in a plastic pot. She saw laundry strung from grey brick wall to grey brick wall, and her world was crowned with the spikes of television antennae and a glimpse of dirty sky. Traffic horns and sirens and burglar alarms and the screams of children eking out pleasure in filthy streets formed the music of her days and nights, punctuated the agitation of radios and televisions spinning fantasies for the inmates of the tenement asylums, underscored by the coughing and spitting of the dying day by day, and intensifying in the sudden outbursts of fighting and the cries of wives and lovers being beaten.

The yellow glow in Sister Esta's muted brown eyes flickered and faded. Her dreams of forests dripping with the silver richness of Spanish moss gave way to a reality of feet pounding upwards for five flights. Four of her six children burst into the kitchen, hungry. The air was still as death, the walls were sweating, and the tired mother gave her fullness of body and mind to the needs of bright-eyed children with empty bellies. For Sister Esta there always would be children. The Star of the East glowed in the hunger of their avid eyes. As she fed them her blood sang with a calling. She washed the dishes hastily, then sent them to a neighbor to stay a few hours while she left the house and headed for the park, to consult with the man who dreamed he was Jesus Christ.

On an avenue of glass dreams one doorway spilling the scents of alcohol and darkness leads to another. Something is eternally pursued and everything is eternally lost. On the side streets exotica crowds the shop windows, remembrances of Bali and Korea, Samoa and Columbia, the Yucatan, the Sahara, and the Barbary Coast jostling one another with their spangled allure. Other shops, perhaps more exotic, specialize in underclothes and night-wear for women, offering synthetic fabrics with the feel of silk colored black, pink, gold, and silver. Leather shops sell vests and boots and whips. The shops are crowded, the streets more so. People covet and touch, eyeing one another, appraising clothing and bodies and exposed desires. Here transistor radios grow wild, blooming in the dank and rancid atmosphere of their native habitat, crackling out a persistent beat made baroque by the frills and flourishes of electronic attempts at music. Older men and nubile girls slip in and out of bars, stores, hallways, touching each other lightly, intimately, and in the streets they beckon, follow, come, go.

The hungry eyes grow starved, die, are reborn to hunger once again. Sister Silvia sat perched at the top of a flight of stairs leading to a dress shop, watching the parade of tightly clothed genitals and tightly held eyes. She chewed gum and smoked Virginia Slims. Her hair was the color of white gold and her body was always stirring, as if a pack of playful kittens were chasing through her clothes of bright red imitation leather. Sister Silvia scanned the street with a professional eye. She was never going to dance naked all night again, drenched in sweat, her muscles aching, for the fifty dollars she could earn in an hour, restfully, conventionally but not always on her back. Her roving eye was caught first by a man, then a woman, then a boy. She estimated briefly the expense of their clothes and the need in their eyes, then signaled and strolled jauntily towards a street of cribs, street goddess, pretty, pert, and pubescently underage.

Naked souls bothered her as little as a naked body. In nakedness was innocence, the innocence of greed, hatred, lust, loneliness, despair, contempt, confusion unconcealed. All was innocence as long as it could be seen. Silvia was new to the knowledge of power. It was still primitive, bound to the rawness and terrible drive interpreted by her youth as purely sexual.

She had years ahead of her in which to see, under her microscope eyes, the diseases that plague the human spirit. Those years would teach her to examine, to diagnose, to attempt to cure. The young diviner swayed through the crowds of furtive touchers and peepers, the ghost of Sister Esta in the yet firm roundness of her belly, the ghost of Sister Calliope haunting her silver footsteps.

In days of old Sister Silvia would have been taken with her head pillowed on a mossy bank, a stream singing in her receptive ear, her hair trailing in sun-warmed waters. Or in a tangle of sweet-smelling hay she would have been laid, or in a field studded with jewel-toned flowers, or in a temple of hetaerae, consecrated to beauty and the gods. To Sister Silvia it was a matter of indifference. She was still learning the power, and all the bleak and jaded world of need was to her wise child's eyes still fresh and new. It was still a good way to make a living.

The boy lay exhausted on the bed. A star seemed to be forever glowing within her, twinkling in her mind, darting through her limbs, grazing her heart, shooting like a roman candle through her groin, giving her prodigious strength and lasting power. The boy leaned over and pinched with his teeth her left nipple, and her nipple stood erect with the forememory of milk glands overflowing. She was about to give him another tumble for free, feeling generous and energetic and with nothing much else to do, when she felt her blood sing with another calling. With an apologetic farewell kiss she dressed and headed for the park, to consult with the man who dreamed he was Jesus Christ.

Douglas awoke to find three women sitting opposite him. He saw a mad crone, a dusky madonna, a flippant whore. The sun was setting scarlet and angry behind them, and in the shimmering light they assumed for a moment epic proportions, three icons looming before him, torn from the fabric of time. As the twilight dimmed, he saw again a battered old woman, a faded housewife, a cheaply dressed adolescent. But they had come to him, he knew, because he had called, because he had dreamed.

"I was sleeping."
The women made murmuring noises, answering him, but he could not tell who had spoken, nor what was said.
"I had a dream."
Again the babble of sound, soft dove noises, woman voices.
"I dreamed I was Jesus Christ."

Their voices swirled around him, an intense lullaby, and he felt soothed and sleepy. His dream seemed fulfilled in the unfamiliar rhythms, the gentle cadences of their unhurried speech. They would write a new testament, attesting to the absolute truth of Douglas's visions, and his visions and deeds would be an inspiration to the coming generations. A testament written by women, read by women, cherished by women. The moon rose in the sky. Douglas felt a halo of celestial light glowing about his head, warming the tips of his ears. Serenely he gazed upon the three women, he met the glow of their eyes gazing back. Sister Silvia casually blew a bubble, popped it with her teeth, and resumed chewing, cracking her gum. "But you ain't, you know," Sister Silvia said in a flat tight voice. "You ain't Jesus Christ at all. You're not the type. John the Baptist, maybe. You got that kind of tortured, fanatical quality. We know a savior is coming soon. A Star has been seen in the sky. Maybe you heard about it?" Douglas shook his head, a forlorn gesture of no. "Well, you have to travel in certain circles to hear about the Star. We saw it. We saw the Star. So we're on the lookout for occult personalities. But you ain't the one. John the Baptist, maybe. You know anybody, heard of anybody who might be a Jesus Christ type?"

Douglas was about to shake his head again, the same sad, wistful no, but he discovered he was angry. "Yeah, I know a Jesus Christ type. Just about everybody I know is a Jesus Christ type. Everybody I know is suffering for the sins of mankind. C'mon, girls, we'll go for a walk, and I bet you the first person we meet will be Jesus Christ. And the next. And the next. All around the world. We'll take a world tour. And me. Me too. I dreamed I was Jesus Christ. I am Jesus Christ."

"Don't get so touchy," Sister Silvia muttered. "You see what I mean? All that hostility. That's John the Baptist. You like locusts and wild honey, right? You get these cravings sometimes for locusts and wild honey. I'd put money on it. Now if you had an appetite for fish and loaves of bread, maybe I'd believe you was Jesus. The real thing. But you're the locust type all right. Locusts and wild honey."

"I don't even know what locust are. Insects or something. I don't eat insects. Nobody does."

"Shows what you know," Sister Silvia replied in her most scathing tone, a tone vaguely reminiscent of the nineteen-forties that she had acquired watching the late night movies on television. She tossed her hair. "Lots of people all over the world eat all kinds of insects. The Australian aborigines eat grubs. Grubs. And they like them, too. The South American Indians eat fried caterpillars. They're supposed to taste just like bacon. A lot you know."

Sister Calliope frowned warningly. "Please, Sister Silvia, behave yourself. We did not come here to quarrel with the young man. We came here to examine him. It seems he is not the one we are awaiting. But he is a sign, definitely a sign."

"I agree with Sister Silvia," Sister Esta said timidly, her faint voice growing louder and more confident as she spoke. "He definitely is a John the Baptist type. We should keep an eye on him. He might be aware of the Savior before we are. Definitely the Baptist. He has that missionary zeal. He was going to show us human suffering, you noticed. And he is ambivalent about women. Fantasizes about them yet is hostile to them. Sister Silvia would make a superb Salome. Really dynamite. There's all this static between them already, and they've just met."

"Who are you?" Douglas whispered. His question went unnoticed. The three women were deep in conference, their voices rising and falling in the night air, their tones growing shrill, heated, then subsiding back into the cooing murmur Douglas found so hypnotic. Although the air had no chill to it, Sister Calliope shivered and tightened the wrap of her shawl about her shoulders. "My blood doesn't seem to carry any warmth in it these days," she said apologetically to the night. She opened one of her shopping bags and drew forth some sandwiches wrapped in wax paper. She held a sandwich before her as if it were a wafer, sacramentally, and offered it to the world. "I haven't had my dinner yet. I suppose no one else has either. They're all cream cheese and jelly. I've got lots of them." She peered nearsightedly into the dark, trying to read the polite smiles of refusal. Satisfied that no one else was hungry, she nibbled her way through six of the sandwiches, gumming the soft squashy white bread, licking gobs of jelly from her lips with a delicate pink tongue. "It's grape jelly," she quavered, holding out the last sandwich. When no one took it, she unwrapped it and began to eat it herself. She only finished half, rewrapping the other half and stuffing it back into her shopping bag. "I'll save it for later. For a snack."

Douglas stretched, rose, stretched again. He felt he had maintained his one posture for hours, had concentrated hard on something without ever having understood anything. He was surprised to hear his bones and ligaments creak and snap. His body felt older than he remembered it, yet he was very aware of being young, younger than the three timeless women huddling before him, younger even than the barely adolescent Sister Silvia. He felt as if he were being punished with confusion for his sins, yet his greatest sin, his original sin, seemed to him to be no more than confusion. Forgive me, I was confused, I didn't know what I was doing. Perhaps confusion was a virtue; indeed, it seemed born of innocence. Confusion is its own reward. Douglas didn't know what to think. Thinking further, he realized he didn't know how to think. He felt empty, a vessel ready to be filled. His old familiar sense of pain and outrage was gone. Sister Calliope smiled benignly upon him. "We've kept you too long. I'm so sorry. We wouldn't have bothered you if we weren't so desperate for a sign, any sign. We've been waiting so long, you see."

Sister Esta's voice carried on as Sister Calliope's trailed off, and their words became a chant, a litany, carrying Douglas back in waves of time, so that he seemed once more in church, though not in church at any particular point of his life. He smelled incense. Sister Silvia was waving a stick of incense before her, a mocking smile upon her face. "We've been waiting for ages and ages," Sister

Esta intoned, and for Douglas the phrase ages and ages was made somehow real, the three women wise as eternity kneeling in their skirts upon the ground. He sat down upon the rock, the rock with the plaque rendering in words its geological history. Rock of ages. A melody danced in his head. First the Hebraic melody, then the Protestant one. He felt as if he were damned to blaspheme, to commit sacrilege with every breath he took. Wishing he were dead, he surreptitiously made the sign of the cross with his thumb upon his belly. "Oh, there have been prophets," Sister Esta continued, "prophets and sages and teachers of men, but not a savior, never the savior. We have dedicated ourselves to the savior, we exist for a savior. Any promise of his coming we immediately investigate, hoping against hope that it is he. But it never is. It would be so nice if we three were the ones to discover him. It would really count, you know. We have been waiting, we have waited, we are waiting, we will wait, through the ages we wait, the ages, the ages...." Sister Esta ground to a stop. She seemed exhausted. Sister Calliope put a motherly arm about her, drew her nearer, shared a corner of her shawl with her, keeping her warm against the chill that rose from within. Sister Silvia drew the shape of the cross in the air with her stick of incense. "Keeps the insects away," she told Douglas solemnly. A quirk of a smile twisted the corners of her lips. "We'll be leaving now," Sister Calliope sighed. "I hope we didn't disturb you. We didn't mean to keep you so long."

"No, wait," Douglas panicked. "There are questions I want to ask."

"There are questions he wants to ask," drawled Sister Silvia. "The wise sisters know all. Do you want your fortune told?"

"There are questions I want to ask." Douglas was an instant away from suffocation. His face was suffused with blood, his eyes bulged. Sister Calliope smiled at him reassuringly. Breath flowed back into his lungs.

"We're in no hurry. Ask your questions."

There were no questions to ask.

Sister Calliope toyed with the fringe of her shawl, her eyes betraying an absentmindedness, a toying with faraway abstractions. Douglas stood rooted to the earth, concerned with the here and now, the reality of the nightsmell of wet soil, the reality of three wise women who spun the fabric of his human destiny. In the dark their eyes glittered; he watched the kaleidoscopic glow with the helpless fascination of a bird entranced by the awful power and promise within a snake's steady gaze. All the concerns of his life seemed to have rolled off his shoulders, to have been absorbed by the damp and dark, to have disappeared into the mud beneath his feet. He wished desperately to recall but one question, one fragment of the web of turmoil he had for so long felt entrapped by. One question, one answer, one proof to carry home with him, locked into his mind, that this night was not dream, not madness, but pure vision, with the sureness of answer that vision means.

"Do you want to know about birth? Death? Rebirth? Afterlife?" Sister Calliope prompted him, her voice gentle and empty of mockery.
"No. No, I don't think so." Douglas felt nauseous, dizzy, unable to concentrate.
"Fate and freedom? Reality and illusion? Man and the universe? The macrocosm and the microcosm? God? We have all the answers," Sister Esta offered, a singsong catechism of wares. She looked startlingly like the woman, strong-bodied and mad-eyed, who trudged through the backyards of Douglas's childhood, buying and selling secondhand goods, her baby carriage stuffed with rubbish. Overwhelmed by a growing vertigo, Douglas sat upon the rock, let his head sink between his knees, and closed his eyes.

"Love? Do you want to know about love?" Sister Silvia's voice rang clear and brassy, conjuring images to dance ghostly and obscene beneath Douglas's lowered eyelids. "Perhaps you want to know about the validity of love, the power of love, the glory of love? Or do you want to know about hate? Love and hate? Meaning? Purpose? Faith? Strength? History?" Her words, forced from between her clenched teeth, slid effortlessly upon the molecules of air towards him, through his slack lips, passed down his gullet, and lodged in his bowels, reverberating there. Douglas was filled with the Word. "Love" resolved itself into its component parts within him, was digested, revealed itself to be four letters, churned in his stomach. His bowels were moved with compassion; the Word, with ipecac directness, touched his awareness. Douglas rejected love and vomited between his feet. The three sisters ignored the mess. The dizziness passed. Douglas felt clearheaded, strong, newly angry once again.

"I want to know about the wolves!" Douglas roared.

The three women consulted among themselves, their voices reverting to the softly hypnotic babble that had so captivated Douglas. He ignored the dovelike sounds, standing straddle-legged over the puddle of vomit, his eyes challenging the world. His breathing was shallow and harsh, his hands balled into fists. Sister Calliope approached him, a sweet smile illuminating her crepe-y face, her hands still toying nervously with her shawl. "We know nothing about any wolves," she murmured apologetically. Douglas met the mild and cloudy blue of her gaze. "I want to know about the wolves!" he roared again, his green gaze interlocking with the sky of her eyes. Sister Esta edged close to Sister Calliope, extended a work-worn hand in a gesture of appeasement and benediction toward the quivering figure of Douglas. "Forgive us. We know nothing about the wolves."

Douglas's throat bulged, red and swollen as a turkey cock's. His voice was steely and controlled. Sister Silvia, unbidden, crossed in front of the two older women, stood close to Douglas, offering her eyes for him to read. Slowly, as if speaking to a deaf or very stupid child, she enunciated, "We know nothing of your wolves." Her eyes were colorless. Douglas raised his arms to shield his face from unknown light. The colorless eyes laughed. "Wolves. He is offered all the answers to all the questions, and he asks questions that have meaning only to himself. Wolves. Only you know about the wolves."

The laughter was a laughter of words, the rain rained words, the babble babbled words, the tree branches etched the shape of words, the light of the moon shone in a foreign tongue, and Douglas felt his tongue alien within his mouth, felt sound gurgling in his throat, heard the word "Wolves" break forth from between his cracked lips. He was lying, alone, next to a pool of vomit, a vile taste in his mouth, the baying of wolves in his ear, the word "Wolves" tasting of blood passing from his lips. The women were gone. The baying of wolves resolved itself into the passing siren of an ambulance. He wanted very much to go home, and remembered that he was in Central Park, without any money. He felt very sick. He could not remember if he had a home at all, but he knew he had a neighborhood, and that he was far from his own turf. He held his head in his hands and regretted everything. He was overwhelmed with shame. He had not asked the questions. Life had stood trembling and female before his godhead, and he had not asked any questions. The time had come and gone. Revelation was brushed aside as if it were too ugly and small for his soul to contain. Wolves. He searched inside himself for the meaning of the question. If there were a symbolism within the question, it was so private that not even he could understand. Wolves. The only wolf he had ever seen was a forlorn and moth-eaten specimen at the zoo, aged and infirm, given over to sleep, waiting for death to open the door of the cage. Oh, he had seen packs of wolves in the movies, celluloid images of cunning and ferocity, operating in packs, circling upon the helpless, the defenseless, the innocent, the ultimate in viciousness seeking an easy prey. But that had been the movies. The strength of the pack was betrayed by the lone wolf he had seen, in unabashed reality, bedeviled by fleas and restrained by iron bars. The heroic figure of the lone wolf, renegade to the pack, master of icy wastes, scourge of all weaker, lesser creatures, became an absurdity when contrasted with the wolf in the cage at the zoo, taunted by small children and bypassed by adolescents searching for the adventure of coaxing a roar from the caged lion, young and massive, doomed to grow old and asleep and find freedom only in death. Wolves and lions, tigers and bears, fantasies for L. Frank Baum to please little children with. Wolves. Lions and tigers and bears did not roam free in the cities. Nor did wolves.

Douglas arose and stumbled along the path leading out of the park. He had to walk, to shake off the spell that night and trees and light rainfall had cast upon him. He thought longingly, briefly, of the tinsel side of the park, the southernmost edge where hotels and restaurants and lushly carpeted movie houses and fountains and hansom cabs and silk-gowned ladies blossomed, where jewelry stores offered discreet glimpses of glowing splendor upon black velvet and taxis whisked yellow-gold through clean streets. But it would be a long walk home from tinsel, to grime, and Douglas stank of vomit. He headed west and then north, towards narrow crowded streets, grimy neon-lit bars, all-night drugstores. He passed few people going home. It was very late. The people he passed he averted his head from, disgusted with the animal manifestation of life balancing carefully, precariously, on two legs, frail naked bodies sheltered from the world by clothing robbed from other animals, from plants, from chemical changes. And so he did not see the young couple twining arms around each other's hips, or the decrepit and shawled old woman, or the father and mother hustling party-dressed youngsters home, or the work-worn woman of middle years scurrying into the downtown train station, or the leather-jacketed teenaged boy huddling nervously in a doorway, waiting, or the under-aged whore with colorless eyes swinging her hips as she walked, or the old man trying to sleep in a storefront doorway, newspapers under his head. Douglas stared blindly before him, seeing only a dying wolf on the cement floor of a cage, while three mad women sat nearby, holding hands and laughing as the wolf tried to roar one last question, his spittle spattering against the bars, while the stars danced arabesques and painted words in the empty space of heaven.

X. Grail Green

The end of a quest is always a retreat, the old man said.
If the hero lives he retreats from death. If he dies he retreats from life. The boy was silent as one is always silent upon hearing words of wisdom. The old man shared the silence and then broke it, smiling. Do you understand?

The boy looked quickly to the old man's eyes, his own eyes troubled. O yes I understand. I always understand. But I do not believe.

Such passion the old man chided. Ah well it is only words I have spoken and only words you have heard. My wisdom is nothing but my own life. And you of course must live your life?

You are laughing at me? the boy asked.

I'm laughing the old man answered. And you my son are leaving.

Yes.

****

"I like to achieve the impossible." Douglas winked at the counselor and blew one smoke ring through the other. "Like that."

"Like what?" The counselor remained impassive.

"Like the smoke, brother. The smoke, the smoke rings."

"That's not impossible."

"Douglas leaned forward, blowing a haze of smoke into the counselor's face. "Can you do it, baby?"

"No."

"Then, amigo, it is impossible. For you."

"I could learn."

"But you won't learn, counselor. You won't learn."
Douglas pushed his chair back, extended his legs, tilted his pelvis forward. He wore boots. He let his cigarette dangle from his lips, from the left corner of his mouth. He slit his eyes against the smoke. "Douglas pushed his chair back, extended his legs, tilted his pelvis forward. He wore boots. He let his cigarette dangle from his lips, from the left corner of his mouth. He slit his eyes against the smoke," Douglas said.

"Douglas pushed his chair back, extended his legs, tilted his pelvis forward. He was wearing boots. He let his cigarette dangle from his lips, from the left corner of his mouth. He slit his eyes against the smoke. He was wearing boots is better," the counselor said.

"Maybe. It's not as subtle. But I, counselor, am creating this life, this Douglas, this story, and he wore boots. The counselor's legs were hidden behind his hiding desk. Douglas presumed he had no feet. Douglas figured that if ever the counselor wore shoes, they would be black and white saddle shoes with corrugated rubber soles."

"I am wearing black oxfords. Why do you refer to yourself in the third person?"

"I don't. I call myself Douglas."

"That is the third person."

"There is no third person. There is only Douglas and the counselor."

"There is the Douglas in the story, and the Douglas telling the story, and the counselor. There are three people, Douglas."

"Four, counselor. There is the Douglas in the story, and the Douglas telling the story, and the counselor in the story, and the counselor telling the story."

"How many Douglas's are there really? How many Douglas's do you think there are?"

"Tricky, tricky, tricky. These walls are green, the desk is in the middle of the room, you sit on one side without any feet, facing the door, and I sit on the other side, my back to the door. There are windows to the left of you, windows to the right of me. The sermon for this morning is are they the same windows. You know I have feet, for Douglas pushed his chair back, extended his legs, et cetera. He means to be insolent. Douglas is a mean lad. Out the windows are trees, counselor, and lawn. Inside, here in this green room, without your green feet, inside my green eyes, it rains green rain, painting the walls a greener green. Is there a legend about a prince who pretended he was mad, or pretended he was pretending to be mad, or was he really mad or only pretending to be? There is such a legend. Douglas, prince of Denmark, slaughtered his uncle because he was too well bred to slaughter his father, but everyone died before he could grab the old lady and play naughty-naughty before all the eyes of all those who came to see. Do I sound schizophrenic?"

"You didn't answer the question I asked you."

"Because it was tricky. And you won't answer the question I asked you, because it too was tricky. There is nothing to be learned from questions and answers, counselor. Nothing to learn. You too, with your questions and answers, like to achieve the impossible. If you think you've learned something, then you too, like me, think you have achieved the impossible, but the impossible, by definition, cannot be achieved."

"You are a sophist."

"You categorize. Shall I tell you stories, shall you tell me stories? Shall we agree on definitions? Shall it continue to rain green upon this room, shall it continue to rain trees and lawn upon the window? You are living a life, counselor, telling yourself your story. I the counselor now arise, for the dawn has come, rosy-fingered, to my sleeping chamber. The inside of my mouth tastes like shoe leather, like a sewer, like roses, like a cow's asshole, like the afterbirth of a rained rabbit. I ache all over. I feel fine. I have a big piss hard-on. The floor is cold to my bare feet. I the counselor, I the bare feet, I the continuing story. In your story you have feet. Counselor. I, Douglas, in all my persons, am living my life. I tell my own stories."

"I don't tell myself the details of my life as if it were a story."

"You're lying."

"I am not lying."

"You're lying to yourself."

"You think you know what I'm thinking, Douglas."

"I know what you're thinking, counselor. Do you know what I'm thinking? I wish one of us was a woman. I wish we could touch and fuck and squirm and get close and wet. Yeah, counselor, I wish I were a woman. I'm too tough to be a man."

"Why don't you want to talk?"

"I do, I really do. I am talking. I love to talk. I also love to fuck. Can't fuck, might as well talk. Why don't you ask me why I wish I was a woman?"

"All right, Douglas, why do you wish you were a woman?"

"I already told you, amigo. So we could fuck instead of talk. Because I'm too tough to be a man. Because I've never been a woman. Counselor, you think I'm in trouble. You think I need help. You need help. You don't wish you were a woman. Counselor, I make you a woman. You are now a woman. If you was a good-looking woman,

I'd fuck you. I'd love you up real nice. But girl, you is ugly as hell. You look like a man. I know, I know, I remember. I remember your face. Time is up. Right. Right as green rain."
"Time is up." Time is up. "Time is up."

****

Where is time, the boy asked before he left. Time is not up time is not down. Time is not right time is not left. Time is not north south east west. Time is yours. The old man kissed him on the forehead. The boy did not want the old man to see his tears. He bent his head over the old man's hand, kissing it. The old man could not see the boy's face. Nevertheless, he felt a teardrop wet upon his finger. As the boy walked away a light green rain began to fall. The old man sat before his door in an attitude of prayer. Another boy much younger in time was climbing the path toward him. The two boys passed one another in the light green rain. They did not recognize each other. They were not in the same time. The first boy descended the mountain. To his right was a city. To his left was a wild forest. Before him a spring gushed forth out of a rock. He drank the green water and sat at the crossroads in an attitude of prayer. Green it rained upon him.

****

Douglas sat outside the counselor's building, outside the counselor's office, outside the counselor's window, upon the lawn beneath the trees in an attitude of prayer. A light drizzle fell. Indoors, the counselor pushed his chair back, extended his legs, tilted his pelvis upward. He wore no boots. He wore shoes. He wasn't wearing boots. He wore black oxfords. He wasn't wearing black and white saddle shoes with corrugated rubber soles. Indoors, it was quite dry. The counselor, through with a hard day's work, sat in an attitude of prayer, regarding Douglas sitting in an attitude of prayer, regarding the light drizzle. In the late afternoon light the rain was green. The counselor flexed his legs, three times. He considered the shine of his shoes. He locked his desk drawers. Rising, he reached for his jacket, put it on, buttoned it. He walked across the green-walled room upon the green-tiled floor to the light switch near the door. He clicked the switch down. The light stopped shining. He walked back across the room to the window. He looked out the window. He looked out the window he looked out the window. Douglas sat outside the counselor's building, outside the counselor's office, outside the counselor's window, upon the lawn beneath the trees blowing one smoke ring through another. The counselor pulled down the shade. He walked to the door, he opened the door, he walked through the doorway, he turned, he pulled shut the door, he put the key in the lock, he locked the door, he pulled the key from the lock and dropped it into his pocket. The key slipped halfway through the hole in his pocket. The counselor walked down the green-walled hallway to the door that led out to the lawn. Outdoors. A light drizzle fell.

"Counselor! Let's blow smoke rings, you and I. A light drizzle is falling."

"I don't smoke."

The counselor without breaking stride continued walking down the pathway to the gate. The guard let him through the gate. It was almost night.

"It rains green! Counselor! It rains green! It rains green upon my scene. It rains dawn upon my lawn. It rains night upon my sight. It rains upon my pains. Rain rain go away little Douglas wants to play. Go home, counselor! You can hear me! It rains green!" The voice of Douglas rhymed in sound and in silence. Tony came out from Green Cottage to tell Douglas to come in out of the rain.

"Is it dinner time?" Douglas asked.

"Yeah." Tony waited for Douglas. Together they walked down to Green Cottage. A light drizzle fell.

****

A girl came out from the city to the spring at the rock. She carried food in a basket. She knelt before the young holy man sitting in an attitude of prayer by the crossroads. Gravely she unpacked the basket, setting a little white cloth before the young man's feet. Upon the cloth she placed food.

Eat she enjoined him.

Thank you. He ate sparingly for he had taken vows. She folded up the cloth without shaking out the crumbs and placed it back in the basket. The crumbs from the lips of the holy man she saved to eat herself later. It would be lucky.

Go home girl. It is raining. The girl remained at his feet. She threw herself down before him in an attitude of supplication. Her perfumed hair trailed upon his toes. The boy sprang up in horror. What do you want he cried waving his hands before his face. Go away. His voice cracked.

I live in the city. Are you going to the city? The girl's voice trembled with eagerness.
No! No I'm not the boy cried wildly. The city is a sinful place filled with thieving men and wanton women. I'm going into the wild forest there to meditate and to become wise.

Ah you've made your choice. It is a good one. I am leaving the city. We can travel through the wild forest together. That is, she said slyly, if you will allow me to seek your protection, master.

No! No you cannot come with me!

You would leave a poor maiden to travel the wild forest alone, without protection? asked the girl hanging her head. Her hair tumbled over her face casting strange shadows upon her eyes. And I am a maiden, master. I have never known a man.

But why are you telling me all this?

****

"But why are you telling me all this?" someone asked. Douglas and the counselor stared into one another's eyes.

****

Go back to the city, girl. Go back to your home. Go back to your mother and father who love and cherish you.

Alas, holy man. My mother is dead. I have just buried her. At home my stepfather made ugly and falsely brave with drinking wine all day waits to ravish me when I return. Only my mother has prevented him from consummating his unnatural lust, and now she is dead. The girl began to weep.

Do not cry begged the boy. I cannot bear to see a woman cry.

Ah take me with you, take me with you. If you will not I shall go alone into the wild forest alone and unprotected. I would rather be torn apart by wild animals than submit to my stepfather's unnatural designs. She flung herself upon the young holy man, her face a tender blossom wet with the dew of her tears.

Very well. I will take you with me. He pushed her roughly away. Only you must not touch me again. You must never touch me, I have taken vows. He began to walk, never looking back to see if she was following. She followed behind him picking the crumbs from the white cloth and eating them as she walked. He could hear the smacking of her full red lips as she thus ate and he could hear the pattering of her little bare feet upon the dusty road.

Still it seems to me that if you are really a holy man you should be able to suffer my touch without feeling desire the girl said when she had finished her supper of crumbs.

Well I can't. I'm still young. I'm not really a holy man. Not yet. But I mean to be.

O horror. Have you led me into the wild forest under false pretenses? Do you intend to seize me and ravish me now that we are alone, where no one can see us, where there is no place to which I can run, no place where I can hide?

No. Of course not. And you mustn't speak to me of such things. I have taken vows. What on earth are you eating? I ate all the food that was in the basket. Not that I meant to leave you without any supper, but I thought that you were going back to the city, to a happy home and food aplenty. Not that there was that much food, that I could be called a glutton. Not that I'm complaining of its paucity either. It was all right. How you females do chatter on. Women talk too much. What was I saying? Ah yes. What were you eating? Where did you get the food? Are you a witch? Were you sent by the goddess of illusion to tempt me?

I am merely eating the crumbs that were left from your humble meal O master. I am not a witch. Neither am I hungry. It is said in the city that a woman who eats the crumbs that fall from the lips of a holy man will then be rendered irresistibly attractive to any man she then meets. Many are the holy men I have met at the crossroads. Many are the men to whom I have proven irresistibly attractive. It is only by the grace of the goddess of illusion that I am now a maiden.

Well I am not a holy man, at least not yet, so you probably aren't any more irresistibly attractive than you were a few moments ago. Now silence. I wish to hear no more of your frivolous girlish chatter.

A few moments ago the girl said dreamily. Ah time, what is time?

Are you a philosopher that you know such questions? the young man asked respectfully.

Ah master, I am too young in time to be a philosopher.

They had penetrated deep into the forest as they walked and talked. Night darkened all before them. The young master, taking pity on his disciple, decided that in a grassy glen nearby they would rest for the night.

****

"What do you think, counselor? Pretty horny situation, huh?" Douglas ran a finger across his upper lip, more to emphasize his smile than to disguise it.

"Tell me more about this story, Douglas. Who is the boy? The old man? And the girl. Who is the girl? Where does it take place?"

"It's not a story, counselor. It's life. The boy is me, of course. The old man is my teacher, who could teach me nothing. He is therefore a good and wise teacher. The girl is my temptation. My first big tempta-tion. Douglas is the story. Douglas has to be the story, but it's a lousy story, counselor. You are obviously a cardboard character in a lousy lousy story. You know what happens when you walk out that gate, counselor, and I stay behind? You drop off a cliff, man, into nowhere. No where. Do you go home to the wife and kiddies, counselor? Is she a horny bitch with hair casting strange shadows over her eyes as it tumbles across her face? Do the kiddies have flies in their eyes? Show me the photograph of the wife and kiddies, counselor. The cardboard wife and the marshmallow kiddies. Do you have hobbies? A hobby? Interests? Why yes, Douglas, I have many interests. I am very well informed. Eleven o'clock news and all that. Off a cliff, man. You want your story to be real life, take me home with you, through the gate. Into your bed with your photograph of a wife. Off a cliff. You wrote yourself a lousy cardboard life, a lousy lousy story."

"You're trying to get me riled, Douglas. You don't want to talk about the fact that you consider your life a fantasy and your fan-tasies real life."

"You put it up front, didn't you, man? You came right out and stated your lousy little problem. Oh Douglas, the poor lad, cannot distinguish between fantasy and reality. Real fine, daddy. You musta read the book. Sharp thinking. Oh, but you're wrong, baby, dangerously wrong. I might just write you out of my Douglas story, man, right off the cliff, paper dolly. You might find yourself wandering in reality one fine day, lost in the wild forest with tigers behind you, tigers before you, tigers all around you, and the real Douglas, the Boy, the Boy, mind you, up the nearest tree with a ten foot blade in his hand, blowing smoke rings through smoke rings through smoke rings. In the story Douglas crushes your windpipe. Did you know that, amigo? He's practicing. Or didn't you read the book?"

Count your heart beats.

"You're hostile today."

"I'm jiving you, man. I wouldn't hurt a fly. I'm a holy man, counselor. I'm hostile today. Today I don't want to be a woman and go down for you. Today I want to be a man. I don't feel mean, I feel gentle. I'm in manhood today. Dig it, counselor, you got to give me a pass. I need a woman real bad. I can't make that faggot scene in Green Cottage any more. It rains green down there, I'm pissing green, that suck-off and up the ass stuff is bad for a growing boy's health. I gotta get it into some real pussy, counselor. Get me a weekend pass, huh man? I wanna go down to the city and get laid. No trouble. No rough stuff. No rip-offs, no armed robberies, no drugs, nothing like that. Just a little tender manhood, counselor. I wanna dip into some nice pussy, that's all."

"I'll think about it."

"No. The bastard said no. You really want us all to go fag, don't you, faggot."

"I didn't say no. I just said I'd think about it. Don't try to pressure me, Douglas. Give me a chance to think it over."

"Oh shit. I pulled too much of that schizo talk, huh? Counselor, you know I'm a bright boy. Remember you was always telling me I was such a bright boy when I first came here, before you figured that it wasn't doing any good, talking like that. You had me pegged as just a troublemaker, a little disturbed but not schizo. You were right. And I've learned. I'm not looking for any trouble, just a piece of ass. I was putting on that schizo talk. I hear it down at Green Cottage all the time. You got me in with some real lulus. Well, think it over, counselor."

Douglas backed to the door. He stood there with his hand behind him on the brass doorknob, staring at the counselor. "I mean, I know you got feet, man. Black oxfords, right? Get me that pass. There's a tiger on one side and a cliff on the other."

The counselor sat on his side of the hiding desk, his feet suddenly hot and cramped and sweaty in his black oxfords. In the inner pocket of his jacket in his real alligator wallet the photograph of his wife and kiddies grinned at the dark of his real alligator wallet in the inner pocket of his jacket. Far across the green-walled room his heavy boots upon the green-tiled floor the boy stood with his hand behind him grasping the brass doorknob. The doorknob turned. The boy wheeled, pulled open the door and ran from the office, his footsteps echoing down the green-halled walls, clattering down the green-floored tiles his long legs in heavy boots, his insolent pelvis. Outside a green sun blazed in the blue sky. The sky is blue. Counting heartbeats. The photograph in the dark of the real alligator wallet in the inner pocket of the jacket whined the kiddies to the wife mommy why is the sky blue?

"Damn that Douglas," the counselor muttered aloud to himself, there being no one in the room with him, "He left the door open again." The counselor sighed as he slowly rose from his chair, pushing it back. He walked around his hiding desk down the green tiles to the door. He grasped the handle and pushed the door shut. Then he leaned his head against the door. The green door was cool against his skin. He turned, walked back again along the green-tiled floor, put on his jacket, buttoned it. He locked the desk drawers, slid the keys into his pocket where they caught halfway through the hole in his pocket. "Got to get the wife to sew up that pocket," the counselor said aloud. He walked back upon the green-tiled floor to the green door. He gripped the brass knob, opened the door, walked through the doorway, pulled the door shut behind him, let go of the brass doorknob. The door was painted green on both sides.

"Drat," he said aloud, fishing for his keys. They had slipped through the hole into the lining. He fished around in the lining with two fingers until he touched the keys. With dexterous maneuverings of his middle finger and index finger he finally recovered the keys. "Got to get the wife to sew up that pocket," the counselor said aloud. He locked the green door, and then walked down the green hallway along the green floor, jingling his keys in his hand and whistling, as he always did the rare few times he jingled keys in his hand, whistling while jingling the way most men do when they jingle. He walked out into the green sunshine, down the pathway to the gate. Douglas was leaning against the side of the building. He's masturbating, the counselor noticed.

"Just jerking off before the weekend," Douglas said pleasantly as the counselor passed. "Beautiful green day, ain't it, baby?"

****

In the wild forest a jackal howled. The girl threw her arms around the holy man's neck. O master I am so frightened. That sound sends chills all through my body. The holy man with trembling hands unwound her pliant arms from about his neck. I have told you not to touch me. It is not right. I have taken vows.

But I am so afraid holy man. See how my breast heaves. I am breathing rapidly. That is fear. I feel waves of flashing fire here the maiden continued, stroking with both hands the curve of her belly. That too is fear. My heart beats too loud, too quickly. Feel it as it pounds. Swiftly she grabbed the boy's hand and placed it on her bosom. She then pushed his hand from her as if it were a snake, so that his fingers trailed along her hardened nipple. Forgive me master. I forgot it was forbidden for us to touch.

The boy swallowed. That's all right. Just don't do it again.

But I am so afraid.

I will teach you to conquer fear, little sister, to conquer fear as I myself have done. I will teach you a magic that will keep you safe from fear, that will keep you safe from the attacks of wild beasts.

The boy seated himself upon the forest floor. Now you must sit as I sit. Place the heel of your right foot upon the thigh of your left leg, and conversely place the heel of your left foot upon the thigh of your right leg. Thus.

O it hurts. I cannot do it. Help me.

I am not to touch you.

But your master helped you. I know he did.

Yes he did.

We no longer are man and woman, but teacher and disciple. You must aid me. The boy being intelligent quickly grasped the logic and also her left heel. Together they adopted the position that conquers fear and wild animals. Raise your hand thus, little sister, so that the palm of your right hand, parallel to your shoulder, faces me. She did so. Raise your other hand thus, little sister, so that the palm of your left hand, parallel to the center of your breastplate, faces the ground. She did so. Now fill your mind with pure and holy thoughts. The animals will not harm you.

After a silence of a few minutes, the girl said O master I cannot fill my mind with pure and holy thoughts. I don't know any.

Empty your mind.

O it is empty, it is empty. But I cannot help thinking of the violence of wild animals.

Empty your mind.

The girl frowned. She made all sorts of strange and terrible faces. She then smiled beatifically. My mind is very empty now.

Good. Now fill your mind with pure and holy thoughts.

I have a good one! I'm thinking about the mystic union of Shiva and Shakti, their holy god-bodies locked in pure and holy embrace.

That's a good thought. I guess. But you're not supposed to think aloud. Keep your thoughts to yourself. I have my own thoughts to think.

I'm sorry. Demurely she lowered her eyes. But try as he might, the young holy man could think of no other pure and holy thought but the thought of the mystic union of Shiva and Shakti, their holy god-bodies locked in pure and holy embrace.

As the young holy man and his tender disciple sat facing one another, each filling mind with the pure and holy thought of Shiva and Shakti in terrible mystic union, from out the tangled wildness and depths of the forest crept great beasts. As shadows they appeared, their eyes glowing flame, green within gold, their black and orange

stripes muted by the mantle of night. Great tigers stalked all about
the holy man and the maiden, and jackals slinked behind them. Yet
they moved not, nor did they feel fear, for their minds were fixed
upon the many mysteries of holy embrace. The tigers covered the
two, man and woman, with licks of their great tongues, washing
them with tiger spittle. The tigers thrust their muzzles into the laps
of the two, snuffled in the cradle of the lotus. But though the tigers
nuzzled and slobbered, bestowing upon the two young initiates their
rough caresses, so potent was the thought of the pure and holy
embrace of the god-bodies of Shiva and Shakti that the man and
woman meditating in the forest were aware of nothing but their pure
and holy thoughts. In an ecstasy of wonderment and divine seizure
the tigers and jackals found their mates, copulating in a circle round
the master and disciple, a testament to the power of the mystic union
of Shiva and Shakti. Then the beasts were gone as stealthily as they
appeared, leaving behind them and erotic and pungent perfume.

O my aching back the girl groaned. Painfully she unfolded her cramped
legs. She massaged her neck, and then fell flat on her back, raising
her arms over her head and spreading her legs slightly. O that was
truly glorious she sighed. How nice it is to feel no fear. You know,
I have heard stories told in the city of bands of wild men, bandits
and outcasts, who live in this wild forest. It is said that they rape each
in turn and sometimes in unison unwary maidens, yes even matrons
with children, even old hags, all hapless women who wander into
the forest unawares. But now I'm not afraid of them at all.

Of course you're not answered her master. For this same magic that
tames wild beasts surely would tame the most uncouth of men.

Let them come, sang out the maiden. Let them all come.

Hush. Some one might hear you. Besides, you are not to talk to me
like that.

Yes, yes, you've taken vows.

I suggest you meditate once more, girl. Your words are foolish.
O yes. It was such a lovely meditation. And the tigers were so nice
and friendly. I didn't feel the least bit ticklish. But I think I would
prefer to meditate in this position, upon my back, my face turned to
the velvet night sky, my arms over my head, my legs slightly
spread. Master! O Master! I am having a vision! Shiva and Shakti,
twined in a very intricate embrace, one which I would have great
difficulty in imitating, are telling me that we must evoke their god-
bodies with our own pure and holy bodies. Master, the stars in heav-
en are reeling. We must join in mystic union.

****

"Well, counselor, it was one shit weekend for me. Hope you got
yourself a nice little piece of nookie. All I got was a Green Cottage
group leader pep talk on the dangers of homosexuality—homo-
phobic jerk—and one lousy blow job. Your old lady give you a blow
job this weekend?"

"We'll talk about your weekend, Douglas."

"Right off the cliff, right, counselor? You go out the gate and into
your car and drive right off a cardboard cliff. From Friday into oblivion. No wife, no kiddies, no hobbies, no interests, no blow job. Just
this green room, these green walls and green tiles, the green lawn
and green trees and green Douglas from Green Cottage, green sunlight, green rain. I had a shit weekend. I need a pass for this coming
weekend or I'll blow this fucking shithole apart. I'll jerk off in the
middle of that green cardboard lawn and rain enough green come to
drown the whole mess. I'm opting out of your story, mother. I got a
life waiting for me in the forest with a broad who's just dying for it,
man. She's ready to put out for me so bad. I got her so horny with
that don't touch me jive. Weekend pass, counselor. She's got her legs
slightly spread, she don't wear no panties, you can just smell it,
amigo, and she's waiting for Friday night."
"I'll think about it."

"Counselor, counselor, counselor. You better put me in Security House because I am going to bust out of here if I don't get a weekend pass soon. My cock is going to fly me clean out of here, and on my way to the wicked city I'm going to wander into the wild forest, where I'll find a certain cardboard cunt who's going to get one taste of real live living cock before her photograph tears itself to pieces. Hey counselor, give me a break. I had an unhappy childhood."

"Why do you mention your unhappy childhood? You think it's just jive but you want to talk about it. You really want to talk about it."

"Yeah, but to my mother, counselor, not to you. I want her to feel real guilty and hug me and kiss me while I got my hands down her dress and up her dress and snatch me some nice soft grabs while we both examine our tragic past. Is that what you want to do to your mother, counselor?"

"No. No, I don't. Tell me about your mother, Douglas."

"No. Let's talk dirty about your mother, counselor. Let's talk dirty. Let's pretend you're the daddy and I'm the mommy, and play dirty. Wanna hear who's screwing who down at Green Cottage? Which one of us fags do you think is the prettiest? We're all fags, you know. You do know. You keep us fags, man, cause you like us like that. Horny kids, born for trouble, locked up here with no women. You got real fag heads, you guys, locking us up here together with no gash around. On the streets we were dipping plenty. You want us up here eating cock in the shower rooms, right?"

"I'll have an investigation of homosexual activity in the Home, Douglas. It does concern me."

O reeling stars. Shiva, does your heart beat?

Douglas sprang across the hiding desk and throttled the counselor. His hands twitched, strained, sought the windpipe to crush it, to silence the green, the rain, the voice. The counselor in desperation twisted his body, hit the alarm button on the floor with his right foot in its black oxford and brought both elbows down on Douglas's arms, breaking the death grip. Douglas slid over the desk, knocking the counselor and his chair to the floor, and began pounding him with his fists as the security guards ran in. They wrestled him away from the counselor, threw him down, and slipped a straitjacket on him. Douglas went limp.

"You all right, counselor?" asked a guard as he helped him to his feet. "You should have had a man at the door if you knew this kid was the violent type."

"He never was any trouble before," the counselor whispered, wincing, touching his throat with his left hand. "He was talking about Security House for himself just before he attacked me. Trying to warn me that he was in trouble."

Green walls green floor green sun green rain air green-whirling limp hallway limp greenway through levels the points of the compass spin. Security House. Blanketed. Douglas unbound pressed gingerly the billowing green walls. "Padded. Oh man. What will they think of next?" Full tilt into the wall. "Oh mama. Do it again." Bouncing from one wall to another, tumbling on the floor, leaping for the ceiling. Softly green the room awaited his next move. "Counselor! Counselor! Green and soft she awaits me, she embraces me, she bends to me. Fuck the weekend pass, man! This room is woman enough for any growing lad!"

****

In Security House in the green depths of the wild forest the girl stroked with both hands the green hallway of her thighs. O Master do not hesitate. Obey the commands of the divine Shiva and his consort Shakti. The boy turned his back upon the girl. Your posture is indecent, your words are blasphemous. The gods would not command me to break my vow. Begone, witch. Begone, handmaiden of Maya.

The girl, rebuffed, adopted a more modest posture. Do not spurn me she wept.

I do not spurn you. I spurn the forces of Maya working through you.

Do you not find me beautiful?

Beauty and ugliness are illusion. Pleasure and pain are illusion. Good and evil are illusion. So it has been taught me.

But not for me, holy man! I am not holy! I find you beautiful, I desire pleasure with you, and I know that pleasure to be good. Pity me. I am not holy as you are. Keep me warm against the night. Make love to me in this forest of terrors. If you are so holy as not to feel desire, not to feel pleasure and pain, beauty and ugliness, good and evil, then our union can be of no concern to you. If all things are the same, then you can caress me or not caress me. No harm would befall you. But I, I am trapped by illusion. The goddess binds me to her with all her seductive wiles. Pity me.

The boy fell to his knees, beat the earth with clenched fists, tore his hair out from his head. Leave me alone! I am not a holy man! I am young! I still have much to learn!

Learn from me. Learn with me. You cannot thrust aside desire, that most bitter of fruit, until first you have succumbed to its sweet taste. She crept to him, soothed him with gentle touch. He cowered, he whimpered, he lay his head in her bosom. In the green night she was faceless, but her body was woman.

The counselor walked by them. He noticed they were in the posture of love. Just screwing until the weekend, Douglas said, blowing a smoke ring through a smoke ring. No thanks, Douglas. I don't smoke. It's not impossible, counselor. Shiva and Shakti do it this way. Face to face, the cradle of the lotus. Tigers do it like doggies do it.

But I can't, Douglas. She got lost in the green dark of the alligator wallet inside the inner pocket of the jacket. Cardboard rips, anyway. The counselor walked by them. He dissolved greenly in the forest dark.

O witch you have made me break my vow.

All men break vows.

But it was my first, my only vow.

All the better that you should break it, while it is still young and pretty. No one likes to break an old and ugly vow, a vow wrinkled and sterile, dusty and forgotten. Vows are Maya, anyway. All is Maya.

Who are you?

I am the daughter of your master. The young lad toiling up the mountain as you ran down will in a few years break his first vow with me, here in this wild and greenlit forest. And you will be elsewhere yearning other things. Perhaps one day you too will be a holy man with a daughter. No man is holy unless he has a daughter.

Never. You shall never corrupt other young men as you have corrupted me. He sprang across the hiding desk towards her, his fingers closing upon her windpipe. She was small and tender, woman-rough, and made no resistance to his advances. He killed her easily. As he lay sprawled across her, his breath warming her still lips, her voice sang gentle in his ear. Violence. Union. Murder. I am yet a maiden, I am still alive. In another greenness of time I am at a crossroads, offering food to a young man come down from a mountain. Now, holy man, and only now, can you begin your quest.

In the position that conquers fear and other wild animals he sat meditating on the mutual destruction of Shiva and Shakti, while jackals

159

ate her body. Curled in a corner of Security House he slept, and he slept on until once more he was set free under the green sun with ground privileges and the counselor. He escaped.

City streets. Heartbeat, freedom. Lost, found. Streets. A maze well worth the bull's heart beating at the never centering. Free for violence, for union, for murder, for birth. From the mountain to the forest to the city he slept.

****

"Let me use your works, Brian."

"You wanna buy works? I got a friend works in a hospital." Brian handed his needle and syringe over to Douglas. "How'd you get out, man?"

"Made it over the wall. I got ripped up some by the barbed wire. Here, see? And here."

"Jesus. You oughta have a doctor look at that. That's all infected. Hey stupid, clean that needle. C'mere, here's some alcohol."

"Fuck that shit. You gonna carry alcohol with you everywhere you go? I can see you in some hallway, man, cops on your ass, and you won't shoot up cause you don't got no alcohol."

"Man, Douglas, you're stupid. You gonna get a disease that way. Mary, she's in the hospital right now, with hepatitis."

"Which Mary?"

"Mary, you know Mary. That wop Mary. The one with the body."

"Hope she dies." Douglas found a vein, made his hit.

"You just gonna leave that thing hanging in there? Pull it out, man.

Hey. hey! You okay?" Another green room. Douglas grinned back at the green.

"Yeah, yeah, I'm okay. This make you nervous?"

"Yeah, Douglas. Yeah. It makes me nervous. You are crazy, amigo, you know that? Pull it out."

All rooms are green. There is no end to the pain of it.

"I killed my counselor before I cut out. Broke his windpipe. It doesn't take a minute. No sound, no blood. Very very clean. Then I made a little detour before I came back to the city. I went straight to his house and raped his old lady. She was like dying for it. Never was so happy in her whole life. I ripped the shit out of her and she begged for more. I let her give me a blow job."

You really killed him? Hey, take that thing out of your arm!"

"Here, don't get so nervous. Here's your fucking needle. Yeah, I killed him. He wouldn't give me a weekend pass so I killed him. They locked me up in this violent ward, they call it Security House, but I busted out. You listening?"

"Yeah, yeah. I hear you."

You're nodding out. Fucking no-good junkie."

Out on the streets, Douglas looked for the girl he'd met at the cross-roads. He knew he'd recognize her, would recognize her long dark hair casting strange shadows over her eyes, would recognize her hair and the sweet tiger scent of it, would recognize her lips full and smiling desire, and her bare feet dusty in the road. He grew frantic in his search, nodding out on the steps of the building where Brian lived, he grew frantic before he remembered that she'd been eaten by jackals. He sat upon the hood of a parked car in an attitude of prayer, while the skies rained green upon his upturned face. The counselor walked by, carrying his wife in the dark of his real alligator wallet in the inner pocket of his jacket. Let me out, she begged but no one heard and besides he'd taken vows. The counselor blew smoke rings in the holy man's face. "You fucking bastard," shrieked the counselor, "you wouldn't even let me out to get laid!"

"Make a vow," intoned Douglas. "The goddess sends green rain."

The end of a quest the old man laughed and you my son are leaving.

Yes.

After the thunder rolled and the lightning flashed the rain fell down. People ran for shelter. Mothers pulled children into doorways, men covered their heads with newspapers. Above the street women pulled bedding airing in from windowsills, and hastily closed windows. Fresh and lightly green the rain fell. Between parked cars a tiger stalked, his eyes like glowing lanterns in the gloom. The girl's voice whispered in Douglas's ear, Boy, are you not afraid? Yes, goddess, I am afraid. In that instant the tiger leapt, clawing open flesh, sending innards tumbling onto wet asphalt. Douglas fell to his knees upon the mossy forest floor. Hallways. Keening by the side of his own dead body, "Forgiveness, but I'm just a child."

XI. IN THE GARDEN II

Robust and blackbearded, clad in a shabby worksoiled tunic, the carpenter stood in the shade of the pine trees, balancing upon his back his cross. Although his frame was large and his limbs and torso well muscled, he was on the gaunt side, a giant who had lost weight too rapidly. His eyes shrewd, his smile foolish, he stood straddle-legged upon the pine needle-slippery forest floor, his head inclined towards his companion, listening. Had he been a fox or a dog, his ears would have been erect and cupped, straining towards sound. Being a man, or something more than man, his attention showed not in the angle of his ears but in his posture, alert, leaning forward. Occasionally he would reach back with his right arm and shove the sliding cross further up his back so that his shoulders could carry the weight.

His companion, slight and beardless, with a soft, white, feminine body, toyed indolently with his cascade of golden blond curls that reached below his shoulders. Immaculately dressed in a gold-banded tunic of white linen, the youth too contended with an unwieldy burden, and was forced to adjust his wreath of grapevines every few moments, for he had what seemed to be half a vineyard strung about his brow, so that he was nearly blinded by bunches of bobbing grapes. He chattered animatedly, pushing back his curls, wrenching his wreath this way and back, smoothing miniscule wrinkles from his garment, tracing his name with his bare toes in the pile of pine needles at his feet. He had a coy habit of nibbling at the grapes that dangled from his head, capturing them with pouting lips while looking up from under his long, artificially darkened lashes. The carpenter listened patiently, nodding his head in seeming agreement every few minutes, more to let the other know that he was really paying attention than to assert his own identity. The delicate youth was interrupted in his monologue when he choked on a grape that he had inhaled, and as the carpenter pounded him on the back the carpenter also took the opportunity of adding a few words of his own, with effective authority. The boy spat out the offending grape, blushed, albeit prettily, and followed the carpenter down the grassy slope into the meadow. They drew near the glass coffin and the five contending judges. As they approached the five judges stilled their arguments, lowered their waving arms.

The boy pranced about the coffin, eyeing the waxen figure within. "Ooh, Sleeping Beauty," he shrilled. "I swear, your Father's been learning from Walt Disney. Stunning production. Real glass and everything. Hello girls. Out to lunch? Isn't he gorgeous?"

The three sisters eyed him coldly, Sister Silvia going so far as to toss her head. He grinned wickedly, sidled over to her, and whispered, "My hair's naturally blond, sweetie. But you got a very good beautician, I must hand it to you."

Sister Esta strode over to the carpenter, kissed him warmly on both cheeks, and proclaimed, "Immanuel! My God, ain't you a sight for sore eyes. I haven't seen you for ages." Kissing him again, she slipped her arm through his and marched him over to where Sister Calliope stood, too overwhelmed, too weak-kneed, to move. "Sister Calliope, look who's here. It's little Immanuel."

Tears flowed freely down Sister Calliope's cheeks as she embraced the carpenter, and she stroked his knotty arms with her heavy-knuckled hands. "My, how you've grown. But you're so thin. You don't eat enough. Sister Esta wouldn't let me bring my shopping bags along. I usually carry a little something to eat, you know. She said I wouldn't need anything. Not here. But I knew I would miss them. You never can tell when you need something. I carry a little popcorn for the pigeons, a little peanuts for the squirrels, some cream cheese and jelly sandwiches, my sewing box, a can opener, a nail file, string . . . what's the matter, they don't feed you?"

"They feed me, they feed me. Don't worry about me, Aunt Calliope. I'm fine, just fine."

"And your mother, blessed is she among women, how is she? She's all right?"

"Mama's fine, Aunt Calliope, just fine."

"You go to see her every once in a while?"

"Every day, Aunt Calliope, every day."

"She's eating all right? She's not on any crazy diet like you are, I hope."

"She eats, she's fine."

"So why don't you put down your cross, you're going to stay awhile?"

The carpenter laughed, hugged Sister Calliope with his free hand. "I can't put down my cross, Auntie, you know that." Standing with his arm around the old crone he noticed for the first time Sister Silvia staring at him open-mouthed. He caught her eye, and she shivered at the impact of his bold black-browed stare. "Oh," she said.

"Who have we here? Sister Silvia, it must be. I never would have recognized the child. I haven't seen her since she was in diapers. My, how you've grown." He let his arm slide from Calliope's bent shoulders and walked over to the trembling girl. He pinched her firm, rosy cheek and continued staring into her eyes. "You remind me of a girl I used to know," he said in a low, gentle voice. "She was very beautiful. She really didn't look like you. She had hair soft and black as a raven's wing, and it reached below her knees, thick and curling and richly perfumed. Her skin was the color of Cretan honey, her lips were full and red as the rose of Sharon, her nose long and thin and delicately arched. You are obviously from another place, another time, with your hair cut short as a soldier's and as palely gold as the high, small, winter moon, your nose is short and upturned, your mouth thin and wide and pale as an apricot. Yet there's something about you, the way you stand, the way you look at me, that reminds me of this girl, this long-dead girl. . . . Calliope, you remember the Magdalene?"

Calliope cackled. "Of course, Immanuel, of course. Who could forget her?"

"I am honored, lord," Sister Silvia said, and tried to curtsey. Her short, ass-hugging skirt hampered her, so she quickly swiveled her hips instead. The gesture was not in vain. The carpenter kissed her chastely upon the brow.

Sister Esta jerked a thumb at the blond boy, who was stretched prone upon the glass top of the coffin, gripping the smooth sides with his thighs and gazing with mooncalf eyes at the suspended life, the flesh statue, within. "What the devil is he doing here? He doesn't belong in this here garden. Why don't he go back to where he comes from?"

The boy lifted his head and rested his desire-clouded gaze upon her. "We noticed you were having a little trouble disposing of a soul, so we decided to come over and give you a hand. You're being awfully ungrateful."

"Well, I'm always glad to see Immanuel here and I'd be pleased to take any spiritual guidance he has to offer, but I don't see where we need you."

"Oh hell, you don't see where you need me," the boy snarled, sitting up and dangling his legs over the edge of the casket. "You can't get along without me. Since you're conducting this little trial, I'll play devil's advocate."

"Smartass. This here trial is over." She smiled triumphantly. "We've already made our decision."

"You are a liar," the boy shouted, jumping down from the coffin and shaking with fury.

"And you're not going to get him," Esta continued, "You're just interested in one thing. You're a goddamn sex maniac, you know that? You don't care about justice. You're just interested in his body."

"His body!" shrieked the boy. "What do you know about anything. I'm no necrophiliac. It's his soul I love, his immortal soul. His body's all corrupt. It's rotten and worm-eaten and stinks to high heaven. I love only beautiful things. His soul is so fine, so intricate, so unused. He's a virgin, for the love of Christ. I've always been honest, you know me. I have no vices. I'll admit freely that I want him. Give him to me and I'll see to it that he never suffers again."

"Cannibal!" Sister Silvia screamed. "You'll eat him alive."

"Hush up, girlie. Your mascara will streak if you cry. I won't eat him. I'll incorporate him. He will live forever within me. His soul will view all the wonders of the world through my eyes, will taste the nectar of immortality with my tongue, will know nothing but sensual delight living in my body. And he'll have plenty of company. I am tenanted by myriad souls, just like him, kindred souls."

"It's too late," Sister Silvia wept, mascara indeed streaking her cheeks. "We've already made our decision."

"That's right," Calliope asserted, her eyes brimming over with tears. The three sisters wept together, and every tear that watered the fertile earth of paradise caused tiny snowdrops to blossom forth, of purest white, shaped like tears.

"Women," Mumon muttered.

"I didn't think you would acknowledge our presence in the court," the carpenter said, a fond smile playing over his roughhewn face.

"I'm no bigot," Mumon snarled.

"Nor I. Sir." Shogen bowed politely, but no more than politely.

"We didn't think you would interfere," Mumon explained reluctantly. "We peopled his dreams, fired his imagination. Douglas rejected God and the Devil out of hand."

"We were his icons, we shaped his spiritual life. He read Greek mythology for romance, Buddhist teaching for knowledge, German philosophy for power, pornography for pleasure. The Bible left him cold." Shogen caught himself rubbing his hands together, regretted the gesture as offensive, and stuck his hands into his sleeves, where they could do no harm.

"I'm Greek," the boy crowed. "The Greeks called me Dionysus."

"And the Romans Bacchus, and the Christians the Devil, and God knows where you came from, and who your besotted whore of a mother was, but you're a weasely convert with no scruples, and you just don't count, sonny." Mumon spat and landed a thick globule less than an inch away from the boy's pink-nailed toes.

"The human soul is my mother and father and my home," the boy snapped back. "Don't push me, Mumon, for I know you well. You've drunk of my life's blood many a time, you bulbous-nosed red-eyed boozehound. I assumed a form most in keeping with this inane cottage-variety hausfrau's dream of eternity, and I left at home my bat's wings and scarlet mask and brimstone breath. Push me too far and I'll pop you in my sack and make off with you like a schoolchild trapped by Mr. Miacca for his breakfast."

"Sour grapes," Mumon sneered. "That tender stripling is what you'd really like for breakfast. I'd give you a millennium of heartburn, you Asiatic she-donkey's bastard."

"Boys, boys," Sister Esta admonished, lifting a warning finger. "Behave yourselves before you get Immanuel here upset."

"That's all right, Esta my child," the carpenter said. "After all, boys will be boys, I always say. Why, I remember once, I was a little tad no more'n eleven or twelve, thirteen at the outside, and the elders were gathered at the temple, and I, being punky and precocious for my age besides – "

"We've all heard that story before," Dionysus interrupted petulantly. "Even our Jap brothers over here, the true Asiatics."

"Well, I guess you have at that. Ladies, ladies, dry your tears and tell my brother Dionysus and me what fate you have determined for this young man."

The three sisters hastily dried their tears, and Sister Calliope aided Sister Silvia in repairing her ruined makeup. Mumon and Shogen regarded each other uneasily. The decision had obviously been taken out of their hands.

"We have decided," Sister Calliope announced, in a thin but queenly voice, "to consign the soul of Douglas to his Maker, and to the tender care of Jesus Christ Almighty. We leave him in God's hands."

"May the soul of Douglas follow in the footsteps of the Buddha," Mumon caroled in a strong deep voice.

Dionysus, crestfallen, kicked at the side of the coffin, and bruised his bare foot. The carpenter, haloed, benign of countenance, stretched out his right hand. "God bless you all." He shoved his cross further up his back, lay his arm on Dionysus's pearly shoulder, and the two men turned their backs upon the coffin, and trudged off towards the piney woods, the younger, slighter man limping slightly.

"That was a sneaky trick, ladies," Shogen murmured. "Goddamn missionaries all of you. Blue-eyed devils."

"He was in God's hands all along," Calliope stated piously, rolling her eyes heavenward.

"What else could we do," Sister Silvia whined. "We didn't expect those two creeps to show up."

"They're everywhere," Esta explained, "They're practically inseparable. They haunt the world, poking their noses into everyone's goddamn business. Who needs them, I always say. But there they are."

"So we're right back where we started," Mumon said, ready to laugh. "A garden, a coffin, a corpse, a decision."

"And just because no decision will be made the carpenter and the jester will turn up and make their claim, and the suspended soul will be placed in god's hands, and we'll be right back where we started, a garden, a coffin, a corpse." Calliope shook her head and winked at Mumon. Mumon winked back.

"We've dragged in Jesus, the Devil, morality, life after death, a tawdry little Eden, some sex for laughs . . . why can't we get on with the story," Sister Silvia demanded.

Douglas, resurrected, is allowed to live. The storyteller will tell his story.

Shogen, Mumon, Calliope, Esta, and Silvia delirious in Paradise stretch out upon the flower-spangled grass and crystal-gaze through a hole in space into Douglas's city, Douglas's streets. Look, there, Douglas and Doreen, crowded even in the privacy of sleep, together upon the narrow bed they share, their eyeballs rolling beneath their crinkled eyelids, dreaming dreams, Doreen smiling like a child in her sleep, Douglas's fist balled upon her breast.

The stars are shining; on the beaches on the eastern shore the stars can be seen, but in the city the sky is a bluegrey cyclorama, dingy, reflecting the city lights. Look, there, scurrying through the Times Square subway arcade, pausing to stare at the underground store windows, at dull-black hats and record albums, an old woman wearing violet-tinged sunglasses, clutching her shopping bags and muttering crazily to herself. It's only old Sister Calliope, homeless, barren beggar woman feeling the city's pulse and keeping time, a metronome ticking away in steady sanity deep within her cluttered bag. Who will hear the music when the midnight greys our vision and freezes our hearing, tearing the old cathedrals down? Our frail excuses are taken down from the shelf and dusted off, we fill our hypodermic needles with illusion and shoot up, great stuff, la la la la . . .

Who is singing in the greywashed streets? Who is silencing the silent and teaching the dumb to speak? It's only old Sister Calliope la la la la wheeling her organ through the spring-scented streets, coaxing water from the cobblestones, tears from ductless eyes la la la la how many broken people litter the streets.

Doreen turns in her sleep, throws her arm over Douglas, warms his chest with her spatulate fingers. His dreams ease, his fingers uncurl, and he farts.

Look, look there, there, Sister Silvia, simulating ecstasy, shares an orgasm with a man ordinarily good-looking with a two-fingered hand protruding from a shrunken arm resting in the golden glory of her hair. He lays his blood-suffused cheek against her own pale cheek and tries to regain his breath, wheezing, thrusting once more deep into her to catch the last bitter drop of joy left before his penis shrivels, his balls withdraw, empty and cold. There is no moon this night. The chimney that thrusts itself from the roof that shelters Silvia and the stranger pours forth orange smoke, and the incinerator in the belly of the building churns with flames.

Douglas awakens, frightened. He sits on the edge of the bed, relearning his geography in the dark, and then tiptoes naked out into the hall and runs to the bathroom at the edge of the hall, pisses long and loud, and just as naked runs back to the apartment, triumphantly unseen, to sleep and dream till the morning sun hurts his eyes and awakens him.

Look, please look, there, across the bridge, in Brooklyn, at the other end of the waters, Sister Esta rises from sleep, and is also naked, big-bosomed and sag-bellied, pads flat-footed to the bedside of her youngest daughter, who wails as she lies in warm pee. Esta strips the bed, peels wet panties off the flat behind of the little girl, and carries her to her older sister's bed to spend the rest of the night, where she really wants to be. Esta smokes a cigarette in the darkened kitchen, scoops water in her hands from the leaking faucet, drinks.

Silvia too smokes a cigarette, passing it to the man who sits naked and deformed at the side of the bed, angry with her, grateful, anxious to go.

Look, look, the city is alive with life, with a pulse of its own, listen, Calliope's metronome, heartbeat, mad music, taste the air, smell the two a.m. ozone. Close your eyes, nod, there is junk in your veins and the music flows with it, close your eyes, this is loneliness, this is wholeness, this is paradise, paradise enow. . . . Douglas, sleeping, is going to be allowed to live, to awake and sing.

XII. ECHO

I demand the right to pray. Here, in this wherever, now, in this whenever, (caught) this parenthesis of extended being that yields me to myself, leaving me the echo of a voice, answer to the staggering chaos left behind, unformed, unfinished. Genesis, consciousness, and the betrayal that begins with the whisper of an asp, so silent that it seems to come from within the very self. Nowhere, timeless, a wisp of awareness remaindered, teased and awakened by the gadflies of consciousness, guilt, and sleep, I demand the right to pray.

Of no one. I demand of no one. Perhaps I demand of time, as if it is never too late. Or of the universe, that chiming pompous word that reduces all conceptualization to self-conscious mockery. Or perhaps I enjoy my helpless arrogance, my demanding of my right to have been, to have lived Douglas, to have lived, and thus to pray.

I am not sure that it ever happened. I will not be reborn. Let my maker struggle as best as makers can; resurrection is as dependent on my will as God's will, and I will not, and I will not be reborn. God's energy is an outside agitator; living I sought death, and death sought me, and given time to think it over I still kinda like it that way. Symmetry, harmony, basic design. It brings out the primitive in me. With a howl I choose balance, death bracketing life, animal to the end. Leaving only an echo. I am listening to myself. I think, therefore I am, maybe, praying. . . .

Douglas. Character determines plot. Or maybe vice versa. Critics can paddle in the dirty waters, the shallow backwash. With the leisure of eternity's echo, I will be left alone with a leitmotif, a theme, a spiraling da capa . . . music of the spheres indeed. I can't hear a thing. Echoes persist in soundlessness. I think. I am not sure that it ever happened. On with the story, re-echoed. God never has known when to stop.

I am the guy who impassively disposed of a dead child's body, tossing it into the river as if it were thirty-odd pounds of garbage. Which it was. Rivers are a symbol. Make of rivers what you will. Will. Anybody can play God. I didn't say a word of consolation to the mother. Jesus had his Lazarus, but Buddha instructed the mourning mother to seek a pea at every house that had not suffered a death, and when she came back empty-handed, she had learned that neither Buddha nor any gods she prayed to could resurrect her child. What a lesson. I could neither resurrect nor teach. I took part in the hold-up of a drugstore proprietor and the old man died of head wounds he received. At the age of sixteen I killed my counselor, then raped his wife and forced her to perform acts of sodomy upon me. According to one interpretation, at any rate. It all depends on how you read the plot. Or the character. The theme, however, with a heavy rock beat, remains unchanged. Soundless. I seduced a teenaged joysniffer into mainlining, taking his first shot of heroin, and I offered him the use of my common-law wife's body as added incentive. I spied upon his feeble efforts at balling, much against his will. I led him to believe I would gratify his lust for me, and then I turned him off without a glance of farewell. I pimped for my woman. I sold junk. I robbed. I shoplifted for the cheap thrill that it brings. I blasphemed, for I thought I was Jesus Christ, immortal. Remember that this is not a confession, merely a summary of plot. Or character. The diction is straight from a police dossier, but that's so much the better.

Am I alive? Dead? Did I suffer? All I really must do is confront my God. Two will get you ten all my God wants is to confront me. We are each other's revenge. Which is almost another way of saying that hell is other people. But not quite. Fiction, fantasy, creation . . . I could say a lot about myself but I doubt if God will ever get the point. There's that Will again. Will God ever get the point?

I'm not too sure any of this happened. I feel . . . what? A sense of unreality, to use the first available poignant phrase. That dreaded sense of unreality. Perhaps the ink is running out. God suffering from writer's cramp. In the spiritual sense of course.

Can you shut the covers tight upon me? Slam closed the book about the pages, consign me to hell in a basket. Have you read this far? Do I seem real? That image, you know, the arm or leg of a miniscule creature protruding from between the lines, wriggling in the air before you, indubitably alive. Haunting image. At least it haunts me. Or God. Squash it like a bug. Play with it, Tom Thumb, Gulliver, curled in the warmth of your bosom. . . . It doubts its own existence.

Did I live? Was I real? Did I suffer? That is the question. The validity of any human existence is suffering, I always say.

Or conversely, the reader, lost in a book, unaware of his own existence, comes to the Sentence, the words in boldface, **DO NOT READ ANY FURTHER. THIS IS THE END.**

The reader hesitates. A little joke of the artist, the lunatic god in his garret, bored, suffering from writer's cramp. Metaphorically again. Toujours metaphorical. The lifestyle of the creator. Ah, but perhaps not a joke at all. **A DIRE WARNING.** Perhaps. It's all in the imagination. Intrigued, amused, peeved, pissed, bellicose, tremulous, hypnotized, alientated, Will-less, Will-fully, Willy-nilly, whatnot, what you will. He turns the page. Inevitably. For the sake of plot. And finds herself staring at . . . Space, stars, a reeling three-dimensional universe, a new dimension, a patch of cosmos framed by unknown but disturbing hieroglyphics. Sucked in, vacuumed up, she plunges through into the ever-widening void, into a foreign landscape of stars. Nova sun, new horizons. Deep space. Double space. Profound space. And he is lost. Identity is lost.

The hazards of reading. A game. But it happened to me. Lost in a book. Alive and suffering. Hath not a fictional character eyes; if you prick him he bleeds. If you prick him with the right stuff, he gets high. Your hands are bloodstained. Your fingerprints upon the margins of the book are evidence, your eyes are guilty of having seen, of having created my suffering along with my god. I am created in God's own image. Or do you read with kid gloves on? I doubt my own identity. Am I well-drawn? True to life? Familiar? Surprising?

You are a junkie. We all have our own escapes. I escape in, or out, you escape out, or in. We are partners in crime. And saints. You and I are saints.

Christlike.

Doreen. Mona, Freddie, Fatboy, Karen, Harry, Harry's wife, Gloria, Desiree, Aimee, junkies, street people, bystanders, innocent, caught red-handed. God, the Devil, the Fates, Mumon, Shogen, saints and sinners, people, animals, sidewalks, buildings, doorways, windows, alleyways, hallways, stairwells, roofs, airshafts, clouds, stars, heavens, gardens. Edens, parks, trees, grass, dope, needles, veins, rivers. Doreen.
Doreen.

In our veins, in our lifestream, pleasures. Are you stoned? Am I dead?

Don't end the story just yet. There is so much I wanted to say. Doreen began with her salty tears, her hint of dying, with my death. And I dead, resurrected, condemned to having been conceived, lost in some One's mind, blood and flesh unto myself, sacrifice. Sacrifice. Create in my now, my taste of eternity, the closed circle. The garden, the judgment, my fantasy of birth and death, my right to a voice.

A scream among screams.

Douglas. Did you live, a junkie among junkies, did you see with sighted eyes Doreen's room beneath the roof, the city below, did you taste the hunger, the emptiness filled, were you with us all the time, all our many years, our little deaths?

I don't know who I am. My story has been told; in afterword I add my claim to voice, an echo of chapters past. In remembrance, I need to pray.

In other words. I protest. This is a scream, written first in long-hand, then type. Printed, microfilmed, memorized. Echo of a scream. Shriek? Yelp? What do you hear? Hear me. Hear Douglas. Hear Douglas scream.

Douglas. In the middle of a page, doubting my own existence.

Narrator, third person singular. Doubting his own identity. Plural. Doubting their identity. Do you read us?

Please.

Christ-like.

Scream.

Doreen.

Echo.

Identity.

Existence.

Simplicity.

Doubt.

Et cetera.

Let me confess, I wanted to be a saint, patron of a white-joy world, image of ecstasy sensed, sought mirror to need. In bleeding color, sunset of the gods. I find myself dead at the beginning and dead in the middle and an afterthought at the end. That's called structure. Lead me backwards, for I am suddenly gone blind. I promise I won't disappoint you. Who am I? A romanticist. Mythology of pain. A phrase. Mythographer of pain. A conceit. A musician without an axe, lyrical; a visionary without a medium, dispirited; a missionary without a creed, faithful; a storyteller without a voice, squatting before my lack of midnight flickering campfire, silent; in the shadow of shadows, remembering lies. I pray, I protest, once upon a time.

About the Author

Merle Molofsky is a psychoanalyst and author. She is the recipient of the 2012 NAAP Gradiva Award for Poetry. Her poetry has appeared in numerous small press publications, and in 2011 Poets Union Press published two volumes of her poetry, *Mad Crazy Love: Love Poems and Mad Songs*, with an introduction by Paul C. Cooper, and *Ladder of Words*, with an introduction by Lawrence LeShan. Her play, *Kool-Aid,* directed by Jack Gelber, was produced at the Forum Theater of Lincoln Center in 1971, and featured an up-and-coming young actor, Robert de Niro. The two one-act plays that together comprise *Kool-Aid*—"Grail Green" and "Three Street Koans"—were adapted from two chapters in this novel, *Streets 1970*, and the playscripts were published in *Other/Wise*, the online journal of the International Forum for Psychoanalytic Education (IFPE).

Her short fiction has been published in several venues, including the online journal *Moondance*. She has published psychoanalytic articles and book reviews in various professional journals. Her chapter, "Empathy, Identification, and Discovering the Other", appears in *Psychotherapy and Religion: Many Paths, One Journey* (2005), and her chapter, "The Music of Awakening", appears in *Defining Moments for Therapists* (2013). She serves on the editorial boards of *The Psychoanalytic Review* and *Journal of Psychohistory*, on the Board of Directors of IFPE, and the Advisory Board of the Harlem Family Institute (HFI). She is on the faculty of NPAP and HFI. She is former Dean of Training, NPAP, and former Director of Education, Institute for Expressive Analysis. She is married to poet, singer/songwriter, conceptual artist, and Taiko drummer Les Von Losberg, has three wonderful children and six delightful grandchildren.